AGATHA FALLS

CHAPTER ONE

I've always felt like an outsider. Maybe it was my parents fault for moving us from Chicago to this boring town in the middle of southern Connecticut, where I didn't know anyone and nobody knew me. The only friend I made that summer was another twelve year old girl who lived next door to me. Her name was Melissa. She didn't have any friends either because she was fat and had a lisp. We spent a lot of our time outdoors and the forest was our playground. Our favorite game was to walk the waterfall near our home.

Thinking back now, we must have done it hundreds of times during the summer before seventh grade. I guess when you're twelve you think you're invincible. We knew the secret. We would walk very slowly, facing the water with our knees slightly bent. It worked every time.

With a 165 foot drop on one side and the rushing river on the other, you had to concentrate. Slow and steady was our style. The Westford River was more than a half mile wide but narrowed considerably toward the shallowest part at the drop-off.

1

One day, toward the end of summer, I became overconfident and decided to run straight across even though my best friend begged me not to. Halfway, I slipped. When I tried to stand up, I found that my foot had caught in a little hole. There was probably a rock there at one time but had since washed away. The more I wiggled my foot, the deeper I sank down into the sediment. I panicked and really started to pull my foot out and eventually I toppled over into the river. If Melissa had not shown up just in time to drag me away, I'm sure I'd have gone over the side. My ankle was sprained and it took us almost an hour to get home. I limped all the way there with my friend supporting me. When my mother saw me limping, she started asking questions. So, I lied.

I made up an excuse that sounded plausible. I told her that Melissa and I had slipped off the Evergreen Cascade. The Cascade was a little collection of rocks much farther down from the waterfall that flowed into a pretty stream. It was so harmless that Girl Scout troops camped there. She believed me.

I think about this every time I walk by the falls on my way to class. I've never told anyone that story. Sometimes, it's best to keep things to yourself. You see, a teenage girl was found dead last week in the Old North Woods about 10 miles from where I live. She was strangled.

We haven't had a murder here since 1981 when a local woman was shot and killed by her husband after she left him for another man. As you can imagine; the town is pretty shaken up about this recent murder; especially with it being peak tourist season.

2

Her name was Joey Taylor. A junior at Evergreen High School, she lived with her mom and little sister on Water Street, the oldest and poorest part of town. All the newer homes are on the Southside where I live.

I'm studying journalism and I want to write this story. The first thing I did was read everything I could find on the murder itself and the act of strangulation. I scoured the internet. I even spoke to the police. What a waste of time. Since I write for the college paper, I used that for my cover. But, the police didn't say very much, using the excuse that it was an ongoing investigation. But frankly, I don't think they have a clue.

So, I made friends with Dolores, an older woman who worked in Police Archives in the basement of the police station. She's been there for years and she's kind of a fixture by now. She was widowed and had three cats. Her husband was former police sergeant so she knew how cops operate. I got her attention by complementing the pictures of her cats taped to the wall over her computer.

I had put down my cat Sasha the summer before so we commiserated about that. Then we went to lunch. I got her to spill and it didn't take much.

Over our lunch of salad and lemonade, well, I had the lemonade and salad and Dolores just had a Manhattan, Dolores told me the cops believe that the killer is a local because of where the victim was killed. No one goes to the Old North Woods anymore. It's not on any of the newer maps so it isn't likely that a tourist

3

would know how to find it. She wasn't dumped there either. So Joey went there willingly. She knew her killer. The FBI has been called in to rule out a serial killer since a student was strangled at Yale last month.

Dolores was able to smuggle me a copy of the police and the coroner's report. The crime scene photos were very graphic. They show a girl with blood red eyes. I learned from my research that when a person is strangled, all the blood is forced into the whites of their eyes. It's very gruesome. There were bruises on her neck where the killer's thumbs pressed into her. From the position of the thumbs, he must have choked her from behind. I asked Dolores about this and she quickly got up and walked over behind me. She put her hands on my neck and started choking me, very gently; but still choking me. I automatically put my hands to my neck.

I could feel her thumbs pressing into my skin. I almost panicked. You can imagine the looks on the faces of the other patrons of Polly's Diner on Main Street. Eventually Dolores stopped choking me and very primly sat down smoothing her grey flannel skirt and crossing her legs.

The feelings of being strangled were not like anything I could have imagined. It was awful. You feel helpless I had researched what a strangling death would feel like. It depends on the killer. If they want it to be slow and agonizing; then the death would be too. I wondered what kind Joey had.

There was very little forensic evidence found at the scene. There were no discernable foot prints near the body either. Her larynx and trachea were both crushed though. That takes some strength. Strangling is usually a guy's thing - not that women can't do it, but it's usually a man who chooses this way to kill. The coroner estimated that she died sometime after midnight.

Her body was found the next day by a local retired couple walking their dogs. The toxicology report came back negative for drugs, so she was clean. Her cell phone was retrieved and now her calls and texts are being examined.

Well, that's enough to start with. My best tactic was to draw the killer out if they were in fact, local. And the best way to do that was to start a rumor that evidence was found in the woods. I was very vague. A small town like Agatha Falls runs on gossip. My best hope was that the killer would hear the gossip, get spooked, and return to the scene of the crime. Killers often do.

It's easy to drop hints since I work at the Coffee Shoppe near the college and everyone goes there. It was only a matter of time before he showed up in the woods. And that's exactly what happened.

Every night, I waited in the woods, to see if he'd show up. Finally on the fifth night, he came. I was hiding in a tree far above the murder spot so he couldn't see me.

I saw a flashlight coming toward me from the woods. I never heard a car so he must have come on foot.

I saw a man walking slowly, flashlight in hand. He knew exactly where to go. The specific location was never mentioned by the local media so it had to be him. He went straight there. He bent down and started looking for something. He was like that for at least five minutes or so until he finally took a nearby branch and swept away all signs of his footprints. Then, he walked slowly back into the forest. He took his time and the scariest thing about it - he seemed calm. He didn't rush. He wasn't afraid of being caught. That means he had confidence.

I climbed down and followed him. He walked to a truck parked a mile from the main road. It was too dark to see the license plate number. I went back to the site where the body was found. The night was humid but the wind had picked up. The odd thing about the wind; it was focused on this spot of the forest only.

I stood for a few moments longer until I got this feeling that I was being watched, so I started for home. As I got to the main road, I swear, out of the corner of my eye, I saw a girl. Not just any girl, but one who had been murdered. But when I turned around, she was gone.

CHAPTER TWO

I missed the bus again. That means I'd have to walk home. It was late October, the days were sunny, the nights were cool, and the humidity of summer had thankfully passed. Halloween was next week. I've always liked Halloween because I love horror films, especially the old vampire movies made in the 1960's. They never gave me nightmares or caused me to lose sleep because I knew that there was no such thing as vampires. I knew the real monsters in this world didn't look like that; they looked like us – human.

My name is Freya Barrett. My mom named me after the Norse goddess of love and fertility. I laugh when I think of that considering I hadn't been out with a guy since my last boyfriend broke up with me. My mom wanted a little girl and had a hard time getting pregnant so when I came along, she thought that name was appropriate. My mom was a romantic.

I had enough money saved for a car when I graduated high school but I shattered my knee playing field hockey. Our medical insurance didn't pay for all the physical therapy I needed so my car money had to go for that instead.

My mom, Rita, was a European history professor with a focus on the Renaissance. My dad,

David, was an electrical engineer but took to teaching engineering once he was diagnosed with a weak heart. That's not what killed him though. A drunk driver took care of that. My parents were driving home from an out of town conference and were hit head on by an intoxicated man who had fallen asleep at the wheel. Both my parents died instantly. Or that's what the coroner told me. But I knew there was no such thing. That's just something they tell the families to make them feel better.

The driver lived and my parents died. Sometimes life was like that. The wrong thing happens and there is nothing you can do about it. Except, go forward. That's my personal motto- *Go Forward.*

I was nearing the bridge now near the city jail. It didn't look the way you'd think a jail would look. There was no barbed wire or a watchtower with guards or anything like that. The maple trees scattered in the front lawn had the beginning signs of foliage on them. If you weren't from around here, you'd think it was a utility company or something like that.

The water had risen over the past few days with all the rain. I liked stopping here for a moment and looking down at the water. Anyone seeing me would think that I'm gazing at the waterfall but actually, I'm resting my feet. They hurt because I'm short and I liked to wear high heel boots.

There was a man walking toward me and he's looking right through me. I prefer that to the way some men look at me, as if I'm a piece of food they want to eat.

I'm pretty, I know that. But I don't want to be defined by my looks. He turned right now onto Pierpoint Avenue. That's fine with me. I was going straight up the hill to my house. In ten minutes, I'll be home.

I was passing the old house on the corner now. No one had lived here for almost three years, not since the owner died from alcoholism. Everyone was polite and said it was pneumonia-but the truth is- he was a drunk.

This house gave me the creeps. When I passed, by I always saw the upstairs curtain move but when I looked closely, there's no one there. An old Victorian that has seen better days, my brother Jake would love to buy it and flip it but he doesn't have that kind of money. Today, a moving van was in the driveway. The plates read Massachusetts. Some rich person must have bought it. People were always moving here, buying up the older homes, and renovating them.

I continued to walk by and saw two men carrying a large trunk into the house. Suddenly, I heard a large whack. I peered through the bushes that line the walkway and saw the trunk on the ground. There was now a large crack along one side and the bottom of the trunk had smashed. They dropped it. I couldn't see what was inside before they carried it into the house. I watched for a few more minutes until the moving van started to back out. It turned toward town. Then, the garage doors opened and a black SUV pulled out. I tried to get a look at the driver but the glass was tinted. It also drove away in the direction of town.

9

I noticed it was getting dark but I was curious. So, I looked around to see if anyone was watching and then I slipped into the back yard. I must see what's in that trunk. And I've always wondered what it looked like on the inside and here's my chance. The back door was old and warped. I tried pulling it open but surprisingly, it was locked. But, I was in luck. One of the back windows was open. I pulled it up and eased myself into the room. There were no lights on but it wasn't so dark that I couldn't see around. I was in a large room that was once a living room or parlor as they called them in those days.

The room was full of boxes. It was stuffy and smelled like mothballs. But, oddly enough, I didn't see the trunk. I walked from room to room checking out the faded wallpaper and the water stained ceilings. The floors were hard wood and the staircase was one of the old heavy wooden things that reminded me of the house in Psycho. There's a door under the stair case. Should I open it? Do I have enough time? My watch said 5:30. I'd only been there fifteen minutes. I opened the door. It creaked and the smell of mildew hit me. I was surrounded by darkness.

I took a chance and walked slowly down the stairs. It was pretty crowded down here but luckily, there was a light switch at the bottom of the staircase and I hit it. Light filled the room and I saw what I came after- the trunk. It was in the corner of the room. It was so big. I could hide inside it. Do I dare open it?

I tried the latch but it's locked. Of course it is. Then I heard it. They're back. Or he's back or whoever bought this place was pulling into the garage now. I shut the light and rushed up the stairs. When I got to the top, I waited and listened. They hadn't come inside yet. So, I crossed over to the same window I entered and slipped outside. I ran across the yard and when I got past the shrubs to the side walk, I glanced back. I didn't see anyone and the garage doors were shut.

My house was located farther up the hill but I could still see the Victorian from my front yard. My house was a white cape with dark green shutters and an oak-stained door. It sat on a little hill with a plum tree that my mom planted when we first moved here. The old maple tree blew down when an unexpected hurricane came to town. It came straight through Southern Connecticut causing a lot of damage. We didn't use to get storms like that but with the oceans warming up, it happened more and more here. The front yard was sprinkled in perennial flowers and was bordered by lilac trees and hydrangeas.

I lived with my older brother, Jake and we took turns cooking, but tonight pizza will have to do. I had time for a quick shower and then I changed into a Yankees t-shirt and sweats.

My room was the largest of the three bedrooms and it was in the front of the house. My mom decided that since I was almost a teenager, I should have the biggest room. I painted it light green this summer. The purple wasn't me anymore. I still had my Raggedy Anne collection on an antique rocking chair in the corner. The walls were bare except for a poster of the Eiffel Tower. My mom spent her senior year of college there and it has been my dream since childhood to go there someday. My bed was four-poster but I removed

11

the white lacy canopy after my parents died. It just seemed like the right thing to do.

The timer went off so I set the table for Jake and me. We liked to eat together at the big table in the dining room these days. It felt more like a family. At half past six, I heard Jakes' truck in the driveway. His familiar footsteps entered the kitchen. But he was talking to someone. There's another voice but I don't recognize it. It was a man's voice. My brother was standing in our kitchen with a man beside him that I didn't know. He was young, like my brother and almost as tall.

"Hey, Freya, this is Erik Michaelson. He bought the Emerson house on the corner. And guess who the lead contractor is?" He asked smiling.

He was almost giddy saying this. He looked happy. I hadn't seen him like that for a long time. At least since before our parents died. I congratulated him and offered Erik a glass of ice tea the way my mom always did when someone came to the house. Erik refused.

I wonder if he knew I've been in his house. I tried to act nonchalant but since this was my first time breaking and entering – well technically it wasn't breaking since the window was open…

"Erik would you like to stay for dinner? I made a pizza." I offered. He thanked me but explained that he had other plans. His voice was deep and yet soft. I liked it and I liked him.

During dinner, Jake told me that Erik just moved here from Massachusetts. He was a contractor too and specialized in New England style homes. The renovation would most likely take close to a year so he'd be pretty busy. Since I had a part-time job and attended school full-time, I hardly saw him now. We probably wouldn't see each other very much in the coming months. This bothered me but I kept that to myself.

"Well, it's a great opportunity for you. I'm sure the house will be awesome when it's done." He agreed and continued eating. My brother was a man of few words.

"Is Erik married? Does he have any kids?" I asked. Seeing the expression on my brother's face, I quickly said, "Because I babysit. Does he need a babysitter?" I asked, hoping my excuse is convincing.

"Nope, he's like me, all he does it work." He said grinning widely. We finished our dinner is silence. My brother knew me so well.

CHAPTER THREE

To any outsider, Agatha Falls, Connecticut, seemed like a magical place to live. That's why my parents moved us here from Chicago when I was 12 years old. It was your typical New England town with a population a little over 15,000. Located in south-western Connecticut, the tourists came here for the beautiful scenery and the small town appeal. We had the forests to the north of us and Long Island Sound to the south. New Haven was the closest big city. Tourists liked to visit the haunted hotel on Main Street and the covered bridge on the outskirts of town. We had a huge waterfall not far from where I lived. You've probably seen pictures of it in magazines and about twenty years ago, someone filmed a movie there.

The falls, like our town was named after our founder, Agatha Putnam Ingersoll. Her husband was a sea captain and when he died, he left all his money to her. Since they had no children, she invested it in the town and built the local college. It was one of the first co-educational schools of higher learning. Some of her descendants still live here and they still run this town. Apparently, nothing has changed in 200 years.

We had foliage in the fall and snow in the winter. Most of the people born here never leave. They still sent Christmas cards and baked cakes from scratch. There was always someone selling arts and crafts in the park to raise money for a local charity. The fire department sold Christmas trees in the winter for the Red Cross. People looked you in the face when they spoke to you and everyone was on a first name basis, mostly.

That impressed my mother and she let herself believe this place was magical. But, I always thought magic was letting yourself believe in something when reality told you otherwise. And I always believed that reality was far better than fantasy. That's where my mom and I differed.

I heard through the grapevine that my former boyfriend, Stellen Sorensen had just been dumped by his most recent girlfriend. I couldn't have been happier with that news since he had dumped me for her. Monika Jensen was an exchange student from Denmark and everything I'm not –tall, blond, and model skinny. We had been going out the entire freshman year so when he suddenly told me that he just wanted to be friends so we could see other people, I said fine, and never spoke to him again. I treated him as if he were invisible. It was uncanny that the book we were reading for class was The Invisible Man.

Professor Marino was my favorite teacher and I loved his creative writing class. You could tell he liked the book because when he's excited, he spoke really fast and talked with his hands. He reminded me of my mother who was Italian.

He moved here from Rhode Island with his large family and he was a big fan of the horror genre. In honor of Halloween being next week, he had a gigantic bowl of candy on his desk. I think he's eaten more of it than the students have.

"What would you do if you could be invisible?" he asked, hands waving. "What if you could go about unobserved, would it change your actions? Do you think being under surveillance changes us and alters what we do? That is your next writing assignment. Give me 5,000 words by next Thursday." He returned to his desk, which was littered with papers, folders, and candy wrappers. I wondered what his house looks like.

"Professor, can I speak to you for a moment?" I wanted some advice about my idea of writing about the *North Woods Strangler*- my name for him. The police and local papers were calling him – *the killer*. How boring.

"Professor, remember you said to always write what you know? Well, what if I were to write about the local killing of the high school girl? What do you think?"

He looked at me for a few moments. "Freya, I think it depends on what your angle is. For example, are you writing about the murder as a way to describe the crime or the people who are the victim of the crime? Because, I already know from reading your work, that you always show great empathy in your stories. Would you be empathetic to the killer or the victim? Whose point of view would you take?"

"Joey's point of view; I want to be her voice."

"Well, if anyone can take that viewpoint, you can," he said. "Good luck and I'm here if you need me."

The weather was warm today for October; it was 68 degrees according to my phone. Well, so much for global warming being a hoax. I looked for my best friend. We liked to eat outside when the weather was warm so I took a chance and walked over to the Philosophy Building. There's never anybody there.

I found her on a bench under a huge oak tree. My best friend Ali Park was a science major. She had a twizzler in her mouth and waved when she saw me. Ali was Korean-American and moved to Agatha Falls from Los Angeles her freshman year of high school. She lived with her dad who's an urologist in a gorgeous house not far from where I lived. Ali was serious like me. She lost her mom to cancer when she was twelve. She lived at home too and thought the residence halls on campus were dumps.

"So, what's your final assignment going to be? Have you decided yet?" she asked.

I already knew she was writing about the recent plans for the airport expansion. Ali was always writing about the local economy or the environment. I liked to write about crimes or social injustice. I changed the subject. I hadn't told her about my plan to write about the strangler. I knew if I told her about hiding in the woods while trying to lure the killer she'd do something drastic, like tell Jake. So, I kept it to myself. She could read my story when it's printed in the paper.

"No, but it's early yet. Hey, are you still seeing that guy, Lincoln?" I asked her this knowing it would be the perfect distraction. She met him over the summer and for a while was almost obsessed with him. Thankfully, since classes had started up again, she had returned to normal. She only mentioned him if I asked.

We spoke for a while about school assignments and went our separate ways. My classes were done for the day but I had a shift at the Coffee Shoppe, so I hurried over and when I walked in I saw Stellen, my ex, standing by the counter talking to the owner.

"Here she is," said Rob as he swatted me with the apron he was holding. "And she's on time too." He said peering at his watch. He knew I had only been late once and he kidded me about it relentlessly. It pissed me off and he knew it.

"I have only been late once and that was last winter during a snow storm." I reminded him.

I quickly locked my bag in my locker and walked out front tying my apron behind me. Stellen looked like he was in pain. Good. He dumped me, so he deserved it. He watched me for a few moments but I remained silent, wiping down the tables in anticipation for the evening crowds. Suddenly he spoke.

"Freya, would you like to go with me to The Canterbury Club Saturday, December 9th? Nils is having his engagement party there. It's really gorgeous and the food is great. It's on a hill overlooking the golf course." He said all this as if he were trying to sell me on the idea of going with him.

"Nils is already married." I said remembering the big write up in the paper about his uncle and his bride a couple years back. She was named something Russian. Olga? Or was it Nadia? I couldn't remember.

"It didn't work out. This is a new woman he met last summer. Anyway, do you want to go?"

"Why are you asking me? What happened to Monika?"

"She went back to Denmark. And besides, that wasn't serious." He said, putting his head down and suddenly becoming very interested in the floor tiles. "I just thought we could have some fun and my dad always liked you. He hasn't seen you for a while."

That's because you dumped me for that Scandinavian exchange student, I think to myself. I turned toward Stellen and looked him straight in the eye. I'd been waiting for this moment.

"Look, I've moved on, you should too." I knew that was what a mature person would say at a moment like this. But what I really wanted to do was slap his face.

Stellen just looked at me. "Freya, I know I did the wrong thing but I want to make it up to you. You didn't deserve what I did to you. Just come for the food then. They have a chef from Italy. I know how much you like Italian food."

He looked sincere. His large blue eyes looked a little sad too. Maybe he regretted what he did after all. But then, the writer in me took. I could meet a lot of people at the Canterbury Club. Maybe I could learn something for my article. And I could schmooze with the elites of Southern Connecticut; people I wouldn't normally meet. So, I surprised Stellen and told him to text me the details, I'd go with him. With that done, I walked outback to Rob's office and shut the door behind me.

Five hours later, I was lying on my couch with a bowl of popcorn flipping channels trying to find something to watch. The local news was on. They were doing a reenactment of the murder. There was a girl who looked like Joey, small and dark. The theory was she was driven as far as the North Road and then she and her killer walked the half mile to the spot where he killed her. Then a phone number for a tip hotline was flashed across the screen.

Some stock footage of Sheriff Hadley speaking at the City Council meeting was shown with the captain reading, *Local police pursue leads in Joey Taylor murder*. Finally, an interview with Joanne and Emily Taylor was shown. The mother and sister of Joey made a personal appeal to the killer. Now I knew what I had to do next. I was going to speak with her family. If anybody knew anything, it was them. I shut the TV off and went to bed. I had a big day tomorrow.

CHAPTER FOUR

It was Saturday and the weather was expected to be in the high 60's again. I hopped in Jake's truck for the drive to Joey's house. Water Street was located in the oldest part of town and the houses showed it. Many of them were built in the late 1960's when the town really started to expand. There's nothing remarkable about them except that they are all postage stamp sized with small yards. I parked across the street from Joey's house and saw a battered red Subaru in the graveled driveway. An empty metal garbage can was on its side by the front walkway. The house was faded blue with white trim that had started to peel off. There's a blind hanging half hazardly in the front window.

I knocked on the door. A few seconds later a young girl answered it. She looked like a younger version of her sister. She didn't say anything so I introduced myself and asked if her mother was home. She said yes. I told her I'm from the college and offered her my condolences. I explained that I wanted to write a story about her sister. She let me in.

"Mom, there's a girl here who wants to see you," she said this in almost a sing-song voice. She led me over to a couch and I sat down. She told me her name was Emily and she's eleven years old. She asked me how old I was and what's college like. A woman entered. She looked to be in her late forties, at least. But the local paper said she was thirty-five. I guess stress does age you. She was rail thin and had huge dark shadows under her sunken eyes. She looked defeated. From the photos I've seen of Joey, I could tell she didn't resemble her mother. She must have taken after her father, who's out of the picture. He remarried years ago and according to the local paper, didn't keep in touch.

Joanne Taylor worked as a housekeeper at a local motel and from what I could smell, was a heavy smoker. She sat down near me on the couch and immediately took out a cigarette and lit it. I instinctively moved away slightly. I'm not a smoker and none of my friends are either. I turned toward her and explained that I'm writing an article for Claremont College paper about her daughter. I wanted to tell Joey's story.

"The local paper already did that right after the murder."

"Yes, but that was only facts; what grade she was in, stuff like that. I want to write about her. Who was she? What were her dreams? Who were her friends? Did she have a boyfriend?"

"Have you spoken to the police yet?" she asked between puffs.

"Yes, but they didn't say anything new. You know, it's an ongoing investigation."

"I think she was seeing someone; maybe an older man, I'm not sure but I think he's the one who killed her."

I looked over at Emily. She nodded in agreement. "She was going out with a boy her own age from school and she dropped him, just like that. She started acting differently. She suddenly hated this house and our life here. It was like she changed overnight."

"Who do you think it was?" I asked, hoping she would give me a name.

"I don't know. She showed up one day with an antique locket. I could tell it was valuable when I saw it. She said she paid for it with her babysitting money but I knew she was lying." She looked sad when she said this, acknowledging her daughter's secret life.

"Where is the locket now?" I asked suddenly realizing this was an important clue.

"We can't find it and it wasn't with her when they found her." She stubbed her cigarette out. "Would you like to see her room? Emily can show you. I've got to lie down. My head is killing me." She got up and walked toward the back of the house and I heard a door shut.

As I entered the bedroom, it was obvious that this was where Joanne Taylor spent her meager salary. The room held twin beds covered in light blue, pink and white bed spreads with matching fluffy pillows. The walls were painted a light pink color. The dressers were old but covered with lace and the window

23

treatments were those old fashioned balloon shades. The overall effect was lovely. Emily sat at the desk in the corner and I sat on one of the beds facing her.

Kids were smart. Adults forget that when they grew up. I was still young enough to remember being 11 years old. I began by telling her about my birthday coming up and my goal of getting a car. She seemed excited by this and asked me lots of questions about my own life. Did I have a boyfriend? What kind of car was I thinking of getting? She was mature for her years. I liked her.

"So, Emily, what do you think happened to Joey?" I asked. She paused for a moment and her answer took me totally by surprise.

"I think the guy in the yellow mustang convertible killed her." She said matter of factly.

What yellow mustang? What is she talking about? This is the first I'd heard of this car.

"What yellow mustang? When did you see it?" I asked.

"Early August. The same time she got her necklace. It was a peridot locket. That's her birthstone." She pronounced the word, per-I-dot. I almost smiled until I realized what she has said.

"Have you told the police? And how do you know the car was a mustang?" Even I wouldn't be able to identify one of those.

"I knew it was an older car because I like to watch old movies and I checked it on the internet. In fact, I think it was a1965 or 1967 model."

"What did the police say?"

"They wrote it down. But, let's be serious. I'm eleven and they probably don't believe me." I liked this kid. I wanted to help her.

"Did you see who was driving?"

"No, it was too dark."

"Did you ever ask Joey about it?"

She nodded. "Yeah but she told me to mind my own business."

"Did your sister change her appearance in any way during this time? What about hair and makeup? Did she try to look older?"

"No, but she got a tattoo on her wrist. It was really small. My mom had this rule, no tattoos, or piercings."

I don't remember seeing a tattoo mentioned in the coroner's report. I'd have to reread that. "What did it look like?"

Emily's face scrunched up as she tried to remember. "It was a number. I think a 3 or an 8. She wouldn't tell me what it meant."

"When did you first remember seeing it?"

"I think in July."

I left and gave her my contact information. I told her to call me if she ever needed to talk. She seemed to like that and told me her mom wanted to move back to Dayton to be with her family. She had a job lined up out there at her brother's dry cleaning business. It's probably for the best, since there's nothing left for them here.

CHAPTER FIVE

When I woke up the next morning, I saw the red-light blinking on my answering machine. It must be Dolores; she's the only one who ever called my land line. I pressed the button and listened, it was Dolores. She wanted me to call her that was the entire message. I called her and she asked if I could stop over today before noon. She was going to the golf course to meet friends for lunch. I agreed and less than 45 minutes later, I was on my way.

Dolores didn't golf but she did have lunch at Penelope's Tavern located near the golf course. According to Dolores, they served the best Manhattan's in town.

When I walked up her driveway, her fat tiger cat, Columbo, greeted me. He recognized me and started rubbing himself against my legs. I rang the doorbell and Dolores answered in a lovely white cashmere twinset. I walked into her recently renovated kitchen. It was huge and my favorite room in her house. I saw Christie, her little black kitten curled up in a basket in the corner.

"Where's Sherlock?" I asked looking around for the Maine Coon who always hid when I stopped by.

"He's around here somewhere. Look, here's the skinny," she said dramatically. Dolores began to tell me about Mr. Hammond, the handsome history teacher and soccer coach at Evergreen High School who had a history of sexual harassment. Apparently, the police took him in for questioning last night. Last spring a high school senior girl made a complaint against him. She said he told her if she was nice to him, he's make sure she got an A in Physics; a class she need to pass in order to graduate.

He was questioned but denied it. The parents of the girl did not want to go public fearing it would harm her reputation and future, so the School Board had to drop the investigation. She graduated last June and attended college out West somewhere.

The police took Hunter Redding, the ex-boyfriend in for questioning too. In a lot of murders, the first person they look at is the spouse or boyfriend. So far, it looked like the investigation had followed normal protocol. We talked for a few more minutes and I asked Dolores if she'd drop me off at the campus library. She agreed and before she drove away, I thanked her and she promised to keep me updated.

The Claremont Library was originally built in 1819 but had many renovations since then. I headed for the computer lab on second floor. I saw some kids from my Psych class including Brett Parker and Andy Keaton. They were best friends and both transfers from California. They were always comparing Agatha Falls to San Diego and Los Angeles and Agatha Falls always came up short.

Mike had a grudge against me since I turned him down for a date last month. I don't like him; he drinks and does recreational drugs. I think drugs are stupid and I avoid people who use them. Sometimes he followed me around the campus. He never spoke directly to me. And Andy, well, he was so quiet that it was almost not normal. I avoided him. He stared too much. It gave me the creeps.

I needed to research a psychology paper I'm writing on Personality vs. Persona for Psychology class. According to my notes from class, personality is based on our DNA but persona is something we control. It's how we present ourselves to the world. I thought about this and how it may have related to the killer. He or she may represent themselves as nice, gentle, and trusting people in spite of the fact that they killed someone. According to Professor Rothstein, personality does not change but we alter our persona all the time. One might have a persona at work but another persona with intimate friends.

I worked for a few more hours until my paper was done. I also did an internet search on the Agatha Falls murder and the New Haven murder to see if I could find any similarities. I supposed if the FBI profilers didn't think there was a link, there probably wasn't. After all, they were the experts.

But what about a copycat killer; maybe Joey was strangled by her killer as a way to make the authorities think it was the same killer up in New Haven? I pondered that as I walked to the bus stop and as I was waiting, I looked at all the people milling around. For all I knew, the killer was one of them.

The bus let me off at the bottom of my hill. As I got closer to my home, I saw Jake's truck parked in our driveway and Erik's truck parked in the street in front of my house. I laughed when I realized that they both own the same model of Chevy pickup but in different colors. Jake's was black and Erik's was dark blue.

The smell of bacon frying hit me as I walked into my kitchen. "Hey sis, you want a BLT? I'm making one for Erik and me," said Jake as he shoved a handful of Fritos in his mouth.

"Yes," I answered forgetting that I was a vegetarian. Every so often, I fell off the wagon and eat meat.

"Are you going to the parade tonight? I'm taking Lorna. Want to come?" Another local tradition of Agatha Falls was our annual Halloween parade held rain or shine. It started back in the 1950's and usually I went but this year, I'm just wasn't feeling it. I told Jake I'd rather stay home and watch the John Carpenter marathon.

"Who's that?' asked Erik popping a Frito in his mouth.

I stared at him for a moment. "John Carpenter? He's the director of Halloween, the best scary movie of all time." I answered as if he not knowing that was almost un-American.

"Oh, horror movies, yeah, I don't really care for that genre."

I said nothing.

My brother, who knew me better than anyone, saw this and said to my surprise, "Hey Erik, why don't you watch Halloween with Freya tonight? She can explain why it's such a great movie. You can get a pizza. And besides, I'd feel better knowing she wasn't alone tonight, considering..."

Erik nodded and asked what time and my brother told him. Did my brother just get me a date tonight? I decided to accept this gift. I played along, "So, Erik, what do you like on your pizza?"

"Anything but anchovies," he said. Of course, that's how I always eat my pizza. We comprised on a half and half and we agreed to see each other later.

At ten minutes to eight, I heard a couple of short raps at the front door. I opened it to find Erik standing there. He had showered and changed since this afternoon. His light brown hair was tousled and he smelled like soap. We sat and made small talk until the pizzas arrived. Then we brought them into the dining room.

I placed real china plates on the table. No paper plates for me. He noticed this and I explained my rule-paper plates for outside, china for inside. He seemed satisfied with that. We sat on the couch, he at one end and me at the other. The movie began. He didn't say anything until about 40 minutes later when all the killings were well under way. Then he started asking me all sorts of questions about the film. I could tell he was really into it now.

I noticed he'd moved closer to me on the couch. He was close enough that I could smell his after shave now. It was woody and masculine. I liked it. He noticed that I was sniffing so I stopped. Finally, the movie ended. I purposely didn't say anything.

"That was interesting; I mean it never stops- he never stops. He just keeps coming. It's just not realistic though. Real killers aren't like that," he concluded almost to himself.

We heard Jake's car in the driveway and went into the kitchen. Jakes handed me an orange jack-o-lantern filled with candy from the parade.

"Have you heard the latest?" He looked nervous.

"No, what's up?" I asked.

"There's been another murder and this time, they got their head bashed in. The victim hasn't been identified yet but it's all over the local news. All their saying is it was a young female and she's dead."

CHAPTER SIX

It was early November and the weather had gotten colder as if Mother Nature had finally looked at her calendar. Gone were the warm and sunny days of Indian summer. This morning was cold, rainy, and overcast. When I arrived at campus, I had enough time to pick up my paycheck. It should be a good one too with all the extra shifts I'd been working. Bonnie, one of the servers was there and she gave me a little smile. Rob was in his office. I walked out back and gave his door a little tap before I entered.

"Good morning. I think you're looking for this?" he said as he handed me my check.

I immediately opened it to see what I made and smiled. Nothing put a smile on my face like big pay check. Between my tips and the extra shifts, I had enough saved for a really good down payment on the vehicle I had my eye on. It was a brand new red Ford Escape, a compact SUV. I made arrangements to pick it up this weekend. I'm done with the bus and walking home, especially after another murder.

The article in the paper this morning said very little except that the young girl was found by the railroad tracks on the north side of town. Since the trains no longer run here, that was another deserted area of town that only a local would know about. Usually known for being a drug hangout, I wonder if the girl was a user and even if this is related to Joey.

Thanksgiving was around the corner. But Jake and I didn't really celebrate Thanksgiving anymore. Since our parents died, we really don't do the holidays at all. Christmas was really hard for us. So, we celebrated on the small scale, wreath on the door, small artificial tree and few small gifts for each of us. That was all we could handle.

I had my interviews at the high school this afternoon with Joey's teachers. I called Principal Peabody personally and explained that I was a writer for the Sentinel and was writing a piece on Joey. He agreed when I told him it was about her personally, not the murder. That was a partial truth but since I'm not actually interviewing him, he wouldn't know.

The high school seemed so much smaller to me as I walked in. The Principal asked me to meet him in the front office. It's still where it was when I went here only a couple years back. Not much has changed but I've changed. I checked in at the front desk and a couple minutes passed before I heard a door open and I saw a tall, slim, well-dressed black man walk toward me. He extended his hand and I shook it.

"Freya? Welcome back."

We walked into his office. It was warm and comfortable and decorated with soft colors like beige and light blues and greens. He asked me a few questions about myself and what my story was about. I let him know I wanted to write about her as a local teen and what her dreams were. I asked him about her.

He looked uncomfortable but he spoke anyway. "She was a lovely girl from what I knew about her. She wanted to be a nurse, did you know that? She was a volunteer at Mercy Regional. She was an honor roll student and quite a little actress and singer from what I hear from Mrs. Miller."

He spoke for a few more minutes about her and then we walked down the hall to Mrs. Miller's room. It was the same room as when I went here. He knocked lightly on her open door and when she saw it was us, walked over and gave me a huge hug. It was a smothering kind of hug and I couldn't remember the last time I was hugged like that. Mrs. Miller was my English teacher all through high school and encouraged me to become a writer. She was especially supportive of me when my parents died. She was everything a teacher should be.

Mr. Peabody said good bye and asked me stop by before I left and I agreed. Then Mrs. Miller and I sat down in chairs by her classroom window. It faced the forest behind the school and today the sky was dark and uninviting. It wasn't the most enticing view. I began the interview with basic questions like what kind of student was she and what were her college plans, yadda, yadda, yadda, things like that to warm her up. She talked animatedly for quite a while and then I went in for the kill.

"Why would someone kill a girl like that?" I waited.

She paused, "I never liked her boyfriend, Hunter Redding. He is a bully. Mr. Peabody suspended him once for sticking some freshman's head down a toilet. He almost expelled him but his mother begged him not to. But that's just my opinion. Please don't print that."

"No, of course not," I asked her some more questions about Hunter and she told me where he lived. I'll have to speak with him too. She stood up and walked me to the door. I asked her where I might find Mr. Hammond and she gave me his directions.

"Freya, there's a killer out there. He may not like that fact that you are writing about the murder. Just be careful." And she squeezed my arm like she used to when I was her student. I ascended the stairs to the second level that had recently been renovated and now had extra office space and a teacher's lounge. I walked to his classroom but he wasn't there, so I took a chance and walked down to the lounge. I saw a tall, muscular man standing by the Keurig and when he heard me, he turned around.

Travis Hammond couldn't be more than 30 years old. He was very good-looking and reminded me of a local news anchor. He had that same hair style and way of dressing. He was vain, I could tell.

"Mr. Hammond? Hi, I'm Freya Barrett and I'm writing a piece for the Sentinel, the college paper, and I'd like to get your thoughts on Joey Taylor." I smiled

36

and walked toward him. I was glad I was wearing a short fitted black corduroy skirt with black tights and red V-neck sweater. He was looking at me. I could tell he liked my choice of clothing. The skirt was tight enough to show off my figure but still modest.

He asked me to sit down, so we sat across from each other on surprisingly comfortable ladder back chairs. He set his coffee mug down. I looked at it. You could tell a lot about a person from what kind of mug they drink from. But, not his, it was just a plain brown mug.

He smiled at me with white, perfect teeth. And he knew they were perfect. "Freya, the Norse goddess of love and fertility; I like that." He told me that mythology was one of his favorite things to read and that he went to Norway as a college student on a skiing holiday.

"Have you been to Scandinavia?" he asked. He spoke for few moments about his past travel destinations and then I get right down to it.

"Tell me about Joey."

"She was a lovely girl."

"Yes, I've seen her pictures, she was very pretty. What were her goals?"

"I think she wanted to be a nurse. She was a volunteer at the hospital. Have you spoken with them yet?"

I got right to the point. "There are a lot of rumors going around about Joey. So, it doesn't seem unnatural for there to be rumors about other people." He nodded. "Well, I'd like to get your response to the recent rumor that you have been accused in the past of sexual harassment. I understand that the police took you in for questioning and that you are a 'person of interest'. Any comments you'd like to make?"

I waited. I saw from his expression that he was thinking. After a few moments, he said, "I thought you were here to talk about Joey."

"I am but any good journalist would ask these questions. So, what is it? Is Sophia Wilde lying about you and if so, are you taking legal action against her for defamation?"

"Any questions about that can be directed to my lawyer, Ron Rubenstein, he's in the book. And as long as we are talking about rumors how about her boyfriend Hunter Redding? He was an abusive kid and always getting in trouble around here. He had a well know reputation as a bully. Why don't you go and harass him?"

"Did you see any evidence that he was abusive to Joey?"

"As a matter of fact, I did. At the end of the school year, she turned up one day with a split lip. She told me her boyfriend did it so I sent her to the school nurse. Check with her, she must have documented it. Ask Janine Temple." He started to walk out the door but before he did, he turned around and said, "Freya,

38

you're a pretty girl and this murder is dangerous business. I'd hate to see anything happen to you."

Wow, that was chilling. I walked back to the front office to meet with Mr. Peabody. By now, it's dark outside and the school is empty except for a few teachers and the cleaning crew. He suggested I check out Joey's locker. He thought I might want a picture for my article.

I followed his directions and found it easily enough. It was impossible to miss it with all the flowers and stuffed bears and angel dolls hanging from it. There's the obligatory *gone too soon* banner over the locker. It made me feel uncomfortable and very sad so I took a couple of pics and left quickly.

As I was walking out the side door, I heard someone calling my name. It was my old guidance counselor, Mr. Daley. Bald, sloppy and a great listener; he was one of my favorite people at Evergreen High School. I heard through the grapevine he was retiring this year to Florida to be with his kids.

He hugged me and said, "Freya, back so soon?" He kidded me knowing full well how much I couldn't wait to graduate. He offered me a ride home and I got in his car. It was a mess.

The back seat was covered in food wrappers, old newspapers, and homework assignments. He acknowledged this with a wave of his hand and said he'd clean it later but we both knew he wouldn't. We filled each other in on the happenings in our life.

"I noticed that someone bought the old house on the end of your street. They've done a ton of work and good thing, it was an eyesore. It used to be the most beautiful house in your neighborhood too."

I asked him about Joey and he became visibly upset. The father of four daughters and six granddaughters, he was very disturbed by the whole thing. He thought Hunter had something to do with it. He really pushed for the expulsion of Hunter and was against the second chance that Peabody gave him.

"Well, I'm gone next June and then he's somebody else's problem," he said. He warned me to be careful before letting me off in front of my home and I realized that it was the third warning I'd received today.

I turned on the news when I got inside. It said that the local police met with the FBI today to discuss the recent murder near the railroad tracks. The woman killed was not a teenager after all but a 24 year old well-known heroin user and prostitute. The theory was that her pimp killed her when she withheld money from him. There's no connection between this and Joey's murder. Well, I can cross that off my list now. No connection at all. That meant Joey's killer was still out there.

CHAPTER SEVEN

I didn't have classes this morning. I borrowed Jake's truck so I could run errands and buy groceries for tonight. I also needed to stop by Hunter Redding's house and ask him about Joey. With my list in hand, I started to back down the driveway. I saw Erik waving to me so I stopped. "Hey, what's up?"

"Anything I can bring tonight? Jake invited me, do you mind?"

"No, of course I don't mind. And just bring your appetite. Do you have any food allergies?"

"No, I can eat anything." He said smiling at me.

"Great, I'm making Italian. I'm just off to the store now to get groceries."

"Well, I'll see you tonight, at six? Is that too early?"

I told him it was perfect and we said goodbye. As I parked the truck at the Supermart, I heard a voice say my name. It was Lorna Bordeaux, Jake's on again-off again girlfriend. She was parked right next to me. I got out and quickly filled her in on the dinner tonight and asked her to come. This way, she'd keep Jake busy and I'd have Erik all to myself. Since Lorna was a school secretary at the High School and sometimes filled in at the Middle School, I decided to ask her what she thought of Mr. Hammond.

"Stay away from him. He's so horny!" Her large blue eyes were huge and I laughed at her expression when she said this. "I'm serious Freya, watch out for him. And don't ever be alone with him."

"Why don't they fire him if he's so bad?" I asked.

"Family connections; he's related to the Putnam's on his mother's side." she said matter of factly. Well, that explains everything. The Putnam's were the founding family of this town. If you had Putnam blood you could shoot, someone on Main Street and the town council would probably throw you a parade. She explained that his mother is a direct descendant of Abagail Putnam.

"And he's related to Judge Pringle and Sheriff Hadley," she continued.

Well, that must be nice, knowing you could go around harassing girls and there would never be hell to pay. Groceries bought and paid for, I decided to drop them off at home and then stop by to see Hunter. I had a series of questions for him and hoped he would speak to me. I drove by the Taylor's and it looked like no one was home. There was a for sale sign on the front lawn.

They were moving. That was fast. Hunter lived one street over on Maple Court so I drove there.

I found the place. It was a two story apartment house. There was a young man bending over the open hood of a blue Trans Am. I parked and got out. He looked up at me, checking me out. He was heavily tattooed and had very muscular arms. His head was shaved and he was not smiling. His bottom lip was pierced. He eyed my brother's new black Chevy truck.

"Hunter Redding?" I asked.

"Yeah, what do you want?" he asked this as he crossed his arms.

I recognized this as a defensive posture from my psychology class. If a person stood in front of you with their arms folded and feet spread slightly apart, that was a defensive posture. But if they stood facing you with feet together and arms down or palm side up, they were not threatening. Thank you Professor Rothstein.

My voice strong, I walked toward him but kept at least six feet between us. "I'm from the Sentinel, the Claremont College paper and I'm writing a story about Joey Taylor. Can I ask you some questions? You were her boyfriend?"

"Ex-boyfriend; we broke up in July. "

"Why'd you break up?"

"We got sick of each other. Why else do people break up?"

Cynical but true. "I heard a rumor you hit Joey in the face last June and gave her split lip. Is that true?"

"Who said that? That's a lie! I never touched that girl. I already talked to the cops."

"Yeah, I know. And you didn't have an alibi for the night she was killed, did you? You were home alone watching TV. So, if you didn't do it, how did she hurt herself then?"

"She told me she fell off the stage at school rehearsing for Oklahoma. She was in Drama Club. She had big ideas that she was going to be on Broadway." He laughed when he said this. "Ask her friends in Drama Club. Ask Randy, he lives down the street from her. He's in it too. Randy Joyner. He thought she was too good for me. He put ideas in her head. Talk to him." And with that, he walked into his garage and pulled down the door with a bang. Well, he certainly was not going to win any awards for congeniality.

I looked at my list of names and saw that Randy was on it and his address too. He lived on Grove Street so I drove there. I saw a pretty white house with black shutters and red door. I parked in the street and walked up the stairs to knock. After a few raps at the door, it opened.

Tall, slim, and well dressed; a young man answered the door. He was attractive and was wearing expertly applied eye liner. I introduced myself.

"I just spoke with Hunter Redding and –"

"Hunter? You poor thing, come right in," he said cutting me off before I could explain. He led me into his large living room with beige walls covered in scenic prints. He motioned for me to sit down on a large leather sofa and offered me a beverage. I said no thanks and asked if I could interview him for the Sentinel. I explained that I was writing about Joey Taylor and I had gotten a list of her friend's names from Principal Peabody. He agreed and offered to call Becky Granger who lived across the street. She was another of Joey's friends.

He pulled out a lime green cell phone and texted her. I heard a knock at the door within minutes. A petite red haired girl in stylish glasses entered the room. I could tell she's shy by the way she kept her head down.

I started by asking them easy questions about their friend. Randy was a very confident and articulate person and he knew Joey very well. He met her in grade school and they've been neighbors ever since he moved in with his aunt a couple years ago. He also believed she'd met someone new and that's why she dropped Hunter. Even though he believed Hunter to have a violent streak, he didn't think he was responsible for her death. Becky, on the other hand was holding something back; I could tell.

"So, who do you think killed her and why?" I asked. He shrugged. Becky spoke finally.

"I always thought she was going to get herself in trouble the way she played people off each other. She loved drama and loved being the center of attention. She loved attention; it didn't matter what kind."

"That's because she has no father," said Randy.

"Well, neither do you," said Becky.

"I have a father alright; he just doesn't want anything to do with me. When I came out two years ago, he threw me out so now I live with my Aunt Paula." He said this with no bitterness. It was a fact. I knew a couple kids that had their parents do the same when they came out. Some parents just couldn't accept it.

"Did she have any body piercings or tattoos? I know a lot of my friends are into that, was she?"

"She got a tattoo on her wrist but it got infected so she picked it off. It was really tiny like the size of a dime. I don't remember what it was supposed it be and she was real mysterious about it, like it was private."

"When did she get it?"

"After school ended; after her break up with Hunter."

"Where did she go to get it?"

"The Dragon's Lair, on Main Street, I think. That's the only local place to go. She didn't have a car, so it would have to be there"

"Did you ever see Joey with anybody other than Hunter? Did she date anyone else?"

They both said no.

"What about new jewelry?" I asked hoping that they might have seen the locket.

The still said no.

"What about a car? Ever see Joey in a car with someone after school?"

"Just Mr. Daley, he gave her rides home sometimes," said Becky.

Mr. Daley? "You mean the guidance counselor?" she nodded. He never mentioned anything to me about that.

"How often did he give her rides?" I asked.

Becky looked down as if trying to remember. I thought of something my psychology professor told me about memory. If you want to know if a person was lying, watch how they remember something. For example, if they looked up, it meant they were lying and if they looked down, it mean, they were telling the truth.

"I can't remember. Sorry."

"What about Mr. Hammond?"

47

They both broke into laughter. "You mean the Harvey Weinstein of Evergreen High? Not that I'm aware of. She never mentioned it and I never saw him flirt with her. But he tends to like brunettes so anything is possible. Joey was a beauty," said Randy.

They gave me information about the Volunteer hospital program that Joey had joined back in June. She thought it would give her insight into the nursing career she dreamed of pursuing.

I looked at my watch. I had to get to the Sentinel's offices and get this thing typed up and hand it in to Keith if I wanted to make my deadline. I exchanged phone numbers with Randy and Becky and thanked them both. As I walked to my truck, I shivered in my thin jacket. The temperature had dropped. Gone was the sunshine from earlier today. The sky was dark and overcast. I took that as an omen.

I drove over to Claremont College. Keith was at his desk, not surprisingly. He'd probably have a Pulitzer before he's 30 years old. Keith Gordon had something in common with me. He was also a transplant from Chicago. A graduate student getting his Masters in Journalism, he was a black man in a school where more than 94% of the student body was white. I had a great work relationship with him. I'll miss him when he graduates next June. He's moving back to Chicago. He asked me if I wanted to be editor in chief next year but I don't know if I'm cut out for that. It's more of a managerial thing and I don't think that's me. I also don't see myself at a desk job. I really like writing and amateur sleuthing.

I sat down at the desk I usually use so it's become my desk, unofficially, even though I don't have a designated spot in this office. That doesn't bother me. I'm not territorial like that. In less than 45 minutes, I've finished the article. I hoped Keith would like it. Either way, he'll tell me the truth whether I want to hear it or not.

"Is this it? Are you sure?" He always asked that whenever anybody handed him anything they've written, like that old TV show where the host would say, "Is that your final answer?"

"Yes, it's part one in a series."

And then, I sat back and watched him read it. He had a poker face and I hated that about him. Finally, he finished and said nothing for few moments. Then he looked at me and said, "I think this is your best work to date. I like the way you get into both Joey's and the killer's mind. Can you have part two completed by the end of next week?"

I told him I had some more digging to do. He wanted to read it first and have Professor Rothstein take a look at it too. I said good night and I left. As I drove home, I thought about the dinner I had to make. Everyone would be arriving by 6pm. The lasagna was made and sitting in the fridge. All I have to do was pop it in the oven.

At 5:45, I was slicing the Italian bread, the lasagna was almost ready to take out of the oven, and the red wine was chilling. I set the dining room table with my mom's best china. I made my own centerpiece with sprigs of bittersweet from my backyard and stuck them inside a clear glass bowl of pine cones.

Jake was just getting out of the shower. He was surprised when I told him I just happened to run into Lorna at the market and I invited her at the last minute. I'm glad to see him making an effort tonight. I know deep down, he really liked her.

I heard two short raps at the front door. I opened it and its Erik. He was wearing a dark green crew neck sweater that really emphasized his blue-grey eyes. His hair was tousled by the wind and I noticed the cleft in his chin. He walked in carrying a brown paper bag. He pulled out my favorite brand of strawberry ice cream.

"Jake told me this is your favorite." He smiled a shy smile and I thanked him. He sat down on the couch. I had the TV set on HGTV and he immediately became absorbed in some renovation show. I put the ice cream in the freezer, took the lasagna out to cool, and heard a knock on the door, all in rapid succession. It was Lorna.

"I parked behind Jake. I hope he doesn't mind," she said as she walked into the kitchen. She was wearing a turquoise blue silk blouse with a short denim skirt and dark brown tights with calf length dark brown leather boots. Her blond curly hair was all askew from the wind.

"It's really windy out there. Oh, it smells so good in here."

"Lasagna, garlic bread, Cesar salad, red wine and strawberry ice cream with real whipped cream for desert," I said as fast as I could.

"Well, kiss the diet goodbye!"

Finally, at 6:30, we all sat down to dinner. We all sipped our wine and began to eat. An hour later, the meal eaten, the wine drunk and the candles burned down low, we moved into the living room to talk. I sat with Erik on one sofa and Jake with Lorna on the opposite one. Inevitably, the conversation turned to the weather, Thanksgiving, the local news, and Joey's murder.

My story would be printed in the Sentinel tomorrow. So, I explained about my article and my investigation. Jake spoke first like I knew he would. And he was angry too. I knew he would be.

"You wrote an article about the strangling? And how did you find the time for that? And how did you get your information?" He said loudly standing over me." Don't tell me, I already know because you are so cocky. Even when you were a kid, you were always taking chances." Lorna put her hand on his arm as if to calm him down but he kept on talking. "If you've done anything stupid…." He trailed off not finishing his threat and then stormed off into his office slamming the door behind him.

Lorna got up from the couch, embarrassed for me and said, "Let me talk to him." She left the room. Erik shifted uncomfortably beside me.

"Are you going to give me hell too?" I asked sarcastically turning to Erik. He just looked at me.

"No way, I think you're amazing. But I'm also worried for you. Freya, think for a moment, a killer is out there and they haven't been caught yet. What if they target you next? Jake is worried. You're the only family he has left now. Try to think of it that way." Taken aback by his insight, I felt worse now. I had brought this one myself. I was looking for praise and I got criticism instead.

Erik stood up and walked to the front door. He turned to me and very quickly leaned down and kissed me on the lips. It was a very sweet innocent kiss but I blushed anyway. He saw this and smiled.

"The next meal is on me. Let's plan for next week?" I agreed and he left. Feeling a little better, I went into the kitchen and started washing dishes. I was wrapping the lasagna in aluminum foil when Lorna walked in and gave me a hug.

"He's okay, just give him time. I'd wait until tomorrow to talk with him."

She left and I cleaned up and went to bed. So much for my celebratory dinner with friends and family, I thought as I climbed into bed. I put the local news on. There was an update from the police department about the woman found dead by the railroad tracks. There was no link between her murder and Joey Taylor. The FBI had confirmed that the woman's killer had been arrested for her death but had an alibi for the murder last month in New Haven. So,

Joey's killer was still out there. I shut my light out and closed eyes.

Outside the house, a car was parked. Its lights were turned off. If anyone should ask why it's there, the driver will just say that their lost. That's the thing about living in a small town, everyone was always so nice, and they were always willing to give you the benefit of the doubt.

CHAPTER EIGHT

About five years ago, a group of out of towners moved here and bought up a bunch of old houses and renovated them in the old part of town. They even opened up some small businesses there too. This was known as gentrification. Anyway, everything was fine until the outsiders sued the city to eliminate the Ten of Nine Bell.

It was actually not a bell at all but a horn that blew every evening at ten minutes to nine. It started in the 1950's when there used to be curfew. They argued that it was a nuisance and was disrupting their mental and psychological health. The mayor convinced the plaintiffs to put the measure to the ballot and let the people decide. So, there was a special election.

Well, what do you think happened? The vote was unanimous. The town voted to keep the horn. And, one month later, the town council instituted a Ten of Nine Bell in the morning. Three times the horn would blow in the evening and twice in the morning. Soon after, the outsiders put their houses on the market and moved back to New York City, Boston and wherever else they came from.

54

If there was one thing about this town you needed to know; they like their local traditions. That's why I still felt like an outsider, even after seven years. Some people still refer to me as that girl from Chicago.

Today was the day I picked up my new Ford Escape from the dealership. It was red and had a sun roof. It was brand new and all mine. I called Ali to let her know I'm on my way. I wanted her to see it first.

When I woke up this morning, Jake was gone. I looked in Erik's driveway and he was gone too. I hadn't spoken with Jake since Thursday night when he found out my article was going to be in the paper. The Sentinel printed my story yesterday and between the phone messages, texts and emails, I'd received, I was very popular. Even Professor Rothstein said I had gotten into the mind of the killer. That was quite a compliment coming from her.

I made a call to someone I knew would help me. He would do anything for me. Ben Hadley, the sheriff's nephew and all around geek, worked at the local DMV. He's had a crush on me since 9th grade. I wanted him to track down the yellow mustang that Emily saw back in July. If the police weren't going to look for it, than I would.

I took the long way driving to Ali's house. It took me by the golf course and the hospital. She lived in a cul-de-sac in a Tudor style home with an open interior floor plan. Her dad was either at Mercy Regional or at the golf course, so she almost always had the place all to herself.

She was on the front lawn holding a homemade sign that read, *CONGRATULATIONS ON YOUR NEW CAR.* She squealed like a little kid when she saw it and jumped in the passenger seat and started playing with the sun roof. "It's red! I love red!" We visited for a while but I didn't stay long. I had interviews to finish today if I wanted to make my deadline.

As I started to drive back toward town, I took in the scenery around me. Agatha Falls was a beautiful place to live; especially in the fall. We were surrounded by a National Forest and a State Park to the north so that area was very dense and wooded. The Long Island sound; an estuary of the Atlantic Ocean was to the south of us about 45 minutes away. So we had the best of both worlds here. The day was sunny and the temperature is in the high 60's so I put the sun roof down.

I pulled into Elm Street. Althea Thomas lived here. A senior at the high school, I was surprised that she was friends with a sophomore. When I went to school, the seniors couldn't be bothered with the underclassmen. Maybe things have changed. I parked on the street and got out.

I saw the front porch with its cheap plastic lawn chairs and the faded artificial flowers in a cracked Grecian urn. It did nothing to enhance the outdated 1970's contemporary duplex. I rang the doorbell. A few moments passed and a young girl answered the door. Typical of her generation, she had several facial piercings and a tattoo of a bumble bee on her wrist. I'd definitely have to ask her about Joey's tattoo. She looked at me and said nothing. She seemed very bored.

I introduced myself and told her I was writing for the paper. I asked her if I could interview her for an article, I'm doing on Joey Taylor, her classmate and friend. She shrugged and let me in her house. When I walked in, I was in shock.

The house was cluttered beyond belief. There were boxes piled up in one corner, one on top of the other. Every surface was covered with something. Newspapers, magazines, books, DVD's, cat toys, socks, clothes, food wrappers; you name it; it was all in this one room. I could only imagine what the rest of the house looked like. She noticed the look on my face. "My mother," that's it; that was all she said as if that explained this mess I'm standing in. Oh well, I'm going to make this as fast as I can. I looked around to sit but there was no space on the couch. Two full laundry baskets are there. I can't tell whether the clothes are clean or not. That's not a good sign. Althea took both baskets and put them on the floor and sat down, I sat beside her.

"Tell me about Joey." I began.

"Look, I know you're going around asking about her and I saw your story online for the Sentinel. I don't know who killed her but I'm not surprised she's dead."

What a start. With friends like these, who needs enemies?

"Do you think Hunter did it?"

"No, but he's the most convenient suspect for our idiot police force. And if Joey had another man in her life, she's done an awfully good job hiding him hasn't she?" Cynical but possible true, I thought.

"Was Joey promiscuous?"

She really thought about this as she twisted her hair around her index finger. "No, just an opportunist, But in my opinion, that's a kind of the same thing, isn't it?"

Wow, this kid had great insight. I changed the subject.

"Did Joey have any tattoos?"

"I don't think so."

"What about jewelry? Did you ever see her with a new piece of jewelry?" She shook her head. I asked her a few more questions but she didn't know anything more.

So, I thanked her and left and drove directly to the hospital. I had one person left to speak to, Tania Menendez. I knew she worked as a volunteer at Mercy Regional so I took the chance that she'd be on duty today.

I parked and walked almost a half a mile to the front entrance. It's a good thing I'm healthy. I saw from the Directory that the volunteer office was on the second floor so I took the stairs. When I arrived, the door was open. It was a large room full of chairs and a

58

couple of sofas. There was an older lady sitting behind a desk. I approached her. Her name tag read, Deb. That was it, no last name. I told her I was Tania's sister, even though I didn't remotely look Latina.

Deb didn't seem to notice that and started typing something into the computer. To my surprise, Tania was on duty until 4pm. She was at lunch right now, so I headed to the cafeteria. I took the stairs to the first floor. The cafeteria was at the end of the hallway. As I entered, I saw the food and beverages on the right and a scattering of tables to the left. I looked around until I saw a teenage girl in a pink and grey vest.

"Are you Tania?"

"Yes."

"I'm Freya Barrett from the Sentinel and I'm writing a piece on Joey Taylor. Principal Peabody gave me your name because you were a friend of Joey's. He said she spoke very well of you." He never said that part, I embellished. People like flattery.

It worked. She asked me to sit down and I noticed that she has no piercing except for earrings, no tattoos that I can see and wore very little make-up. I started out with a few soft ball questions to get her relaxed and then after a few minutes, I went in for the kill.

"Why do you think Joey was strangled? Who hated her enough to want her gone?"

My question startled her. She was visibly shaken for a moment but looked me in the eye and said to my surprise, "Go to the fourth floor. I'll meet you in the lounge. No one ever goes there this time of day. I'll see you in fifteen minutes," she stood up and left.

So, fifteen minutes later I exited the elevator on fourth floor. I saw a sign for the nurse's lounge and I entered. There was no one there. It wasn't a very big room, a couch, a couple of chairs and a table. In the corner was a TV on the wall. It was nothing fancy. I waited a couple minutes and then Tania walked in, shut the door, turned the TV on, and went over to the window overlooking the employee parking lot.

"You did not get this from me, okay? No quotes. Okay?" I agreed.

"Joey thought there was something going on around here."

"Here? You mean the hospital?" I asked.

"Yeah, she told she saw something when she first started working here and it scared her. She was only staying on so she could catch the person in the act."

"Did she say what she saw or who she saw?"

"No. But she was seeing one of the doctors and she told him and he told her to mind her own business."

"What could it have been?"

60

"I don't know, she wouldn't tell me. I've been here since April and the only thing I think is phony is Mrs. Camp."

"Who's that?'

"She's the bitch who runs the Volunteer Program. She hated Joey. She caught her and Caleb in the housekeeping closet. She wanted to fire Joey but Caleb wouldn't let her."

"Who's Caleb?" I asked trying to keep up with this soap opera.

"Dr. Caleb Trott. We call him hot-to trot. Get it?"

Yeah, I think I do.

"What does this have to do with Joey's murder?"

"Are you serious? Maybe Joey saw something here and that's what got her killed."

That's actually a pretty good theory.

"Where can I find Caleb?"

"He's in the Emergency Department. He's the Director. Tonight he's working in Fast Track."

"Fast Track, what's that?" I asked.

"You know, stuff that's not an emergency. Like a sunburn or an earache. Minor stuff that you don't get admitted for, that's his specialty."

"Where's the ED?"

She gave me directions and I'm on my way. I'm trying to come up with minor problem that Caleb can treat. Now, what's wrong with me? Well, I do have a little headache. Okay, let's go with that and see where it takes me. I walked into the ED and went over to the Triage area. I started speaking with the nurse sitting there.

What a bitch! I thought nurses were supposed to be nice. This woman was a Nazi. She took my temperature and blood pressure and then stuck something in my ear and walked me to a room in the far corner of the gigantic Emergency Department. She told me to take off my clothes but leave on my underwear and bra and put on this paper thin hospital gown. She then shut the door and left. I guess I'm supposed to wait for the doctor?

Well, that was 45 minutes ago and I was still in this room with the door shut and behind a curtain wearing a hospital gown and freezing. There was air blowing on me from above. Are they serious? And why do I have to take my clothes off if all I have is a headache?

I heard the door open. "Hello, I'm Dr. Trott. Are you dressed?"

Is he kidding? Who would sit here naked for almost an hour?

"Yes."

He pulled the curtain aside and I saw big blue eyes, dark wavy hair, and wide muscular shoulders on a tall lanky body. God, I wish I really were sick.

"I understand you have a migraine? Do you get these often?" He started feeling my neck and throat and his hands were big, warm, and strong. I closed my eyes and my head rolled back.

"Are you passing out? You seem dizzy, are you okay?"

"I'm fine." Blushing and hoping he didn't notice, I gave him some made up symptoms and he wrote then down.

I asked him about himself. He wasn't married, had no children, and moved here from Colorado five years ago. He didn't have a girlfriend currently. I could see why Joey would go for him. He was a cutie but a killer? I didn't see it. But maybe he didn't actually kill her but he didn't help her either and maybe that's why she got killed. I got an idea.

"Hey, I'm with the college paper, the Sentinel and I'm writing a series of articles on health care in America, could I interview you for my next article?"

CHAPTER NINE

I woke up early and took a quick shower and popped a waffle in the toaster. While blow-drying my hair, Jake walked into my room. We hadn't spoken since Thursday night when I told him about my article. I turned off the hair dryer and waited.

"Are you going to New Haven today?" I nodded.

'When do you think you'll be back?"

"No later than 5pm, Ali and I have 8AM classes tomorrow." We talked for a few minutes about the weather; it was supposed to be mild today and no rain in the forecast. Finally, he got to the point.

"Freya, I'm really proud of you. I read your story. I think it's excellent. But, please, don't do anything stupid. Leave the detective work to the police and FBI. Promise me, you won't do anything stupid."

I crossed my heart and promised not to do anything stupid. Define stupid?

By 1:30, Ali and I had our shopping done. The weather was beautiful so we parked the car and just walked all over town. We looked at antiques, saw some historical sites and window shopped. By that time, we were starving so we went to a popular local New Haven Italian Bistro for lunch.

Ali wanted to check out the book store across the street after lunch. I did too. So, while we were waiting for our food, I checked my cell for messages. Dolores had texted me. It must have be important then, she rarely if ever texted. According to her, the police had finally gotten a list from the phone company of Joey's cell phone calls and texts. That was all she knew so far. She promised to fill me in when she heard more.

"What are you smiling at?" asked Ali.

I made up some excuse and changed the subject. We finished lunch and headed to the book store. I got an idea and walked over to the classic car section, then the New Age and Psychology sections. Ali laughed when she saw me at the register with my pile of books.

"This is for research," I said. She just nodded. We spent the rest of afternoon talking and shopping and finished the day getting dessert from a frozen yogurt vendor before heading home. I pulled into my driveway a little before 4:30. Jake and Erik were in the back yard and they laughed when the saw all my packages. So, I handed them each a bag.

Erik pulled me aside in the kitchen. He looked very serious. "I'd like you to have dinner at my house tonight. Do you have other plans?" I tell him no, my plans for the evening were recently changed, so I'm available. I don't want him to think I was just sitting around waiting for him.

We walked down the street to his house and entered through the back door. He turned on the lights in the kitchen. A huge room with one side covered in windows that faced out toward the back garden; the exterior lights showcased the new back patio and the recently rebuilt gazebo.

According to Erik, the kitchen was the only room in the house that was completely finished so far. There was a new punched tin ceiling and the original oak plank floor boards had been refinished and polished. The appliances were new and stainless steel but the sink was an old fashioned farmhouse sink in white polished porcelain. The countertops were black polished granite with a black and white subway tile backsplash. The walls were painted a light blue and had white painted wainscoting panels on the bottom portion. There was a center island that ran the entire length of the kitchen and covered in oak butcher block. Two mini chandeliers hung directly above it. The total effect worked; it was a perfect blend of old meeting new. I loved it and told him so.

He offered to give me a tour of the rest of the house after dinner. Dinner was simple, steak and baked potatoes for him but salmon for me since I don't eat beef.

We sat and talked at the big round kitchen table in the corner by the windows. He asked me lots of questions about my article. I wasn't used to talking about my writing with anyone. Ali was so competitive

66

and Jake never asked about it; I almost felt embarrassed talking about my work and myself. But Erik was a good listener and soon I felt comfortable talking about the work I did for the Sentinel.

The night was warm for November so we moved outside to eat and he expertly started to grill the food. I asked if I could help make the salad. The ingredients were in the fridge so I went in and searched the gigantic refrigerator. In no time at all, I had a beautiful garden salad made. I even made my own dressing.

"Is Jake doing a good job?" I asked as we sat sown to eat.

He seemed surprised. "Yeah, he's great. Why?"

"Oh, I just wondered. I never see him anymore. When he's not working he's off for a run or he's with Lorna."

"Well, he does have a life of his own."

"Do you have any family in Canada? That's where you're from, right?" I asked. I don't know very much about Erik and he doesn't offer any information about his family. So, I played journalist.

"Yeah, I was born in Montreal but we moved to Vancouver when I was twelve. My dad's a lawyer. My mom is a nurse."

"Are they still alive?"

"Yes. And I have three older brothers, all lawyers and a younger brother in college studying biology."

"What did you study at school?" I asked.

"At first law, but it wasn't for me, so I switched to architecture and design. I can't sit in an office all day and do paperwork. I just wasn't happy."

"Yeah, that's just like Jake." I offered.

"I know. Maybe that's why we get along so well."

"So, are you going to sell the house once it's done? Or, do you think you'd want to live here?'

"I don't know. It depends."

"Depends on what?" I asked.

"You know a lot of things. I don't like to plan things too far out. I like to take things day by day. Most people live their life for their future and never enjoy the present. We always think we have so much time ahead of us but we don't. Life is so short; we don't often realize that until it's too late." He stopped suddenly and got up from the table. He returned with a dish of brownies.

"I bought these at the Main Street Bakery. I hope they taste as good as they look." He picked one up and bit into it. He gave me thumbs up in approval.

After dinner, he escorted me room to room to show me the rest of the house. There were eighteen rooms in all. Some of the rooms were very small. In order to make them bigger he'd have to knock down the walls. When we got to the third floor we passed by a door without going inside. He pointed to the door and just said –attic. He claimed there was nothing there worth looking at and the floors were not safe to walk on yet. He even took me down to the basement to show me some of the old furniture that had been stored there by the previous owner. Some of it was very old and in bad shape. He couldn't save it but he hated to throw it out. I noticed that the trunk was gone but didn't mention it.

As we walked back up the stairs, I tripped. His arms went around me from behind to steady me but I could feel him holding me for just a bit too long and a bit too tightly. For just a second, I was scared. But then, he let me go and asked if was okay. I gave the excuse that I was just tired from the long day so we called it an early night. I explained that I had an 8AM class the next morning.

As I walked up the street to my house, I noticed a truck parked in front. Not recognizing it, I walked faster, but as I got closer, it drove off up the hill. That seemed suspicious to me so I went inside and shut out all the lights. I sat in darkness by the front window and waited for the truck to return but it never did.

CHAPTER TEN

The phone woke me at 6:00. I answered but they hung up. Since I was now awake, I got up and checked my phone to see if I had a response from Ben. Yesterday, I'd texted him. He had a list for me but wanted to give it to me in person this afternoon. He said there were only a few cars fitting that description in Connecticut but it was better than nothing. He hinted that he wanted me to have dinner with him as a sort of payment for him doing me a favor. I guess sharing a pizza with the guy wouldn't kill me.

On my way to the kitchen, I checked Jake's bedroom. He'd been sleeping at Lorna's house most nights. Yep, the bed hadn't been slept in again. I looked out the front window to see if his truck was parked in front of Erik's house, but it wasn't there.

I popped a waffle in the toaster and started to reread my notes for history class. After that, I went into my closet to pick an outfit for today. I wanted to attract Caleb but I didn't want to come on too strong either. So, I settled on black skinny jeans and a new magenta colored sweater with bell sleeves. I added my 2 inch black calf length boots and some light makeup. I blow dried my hair and added some more lip gloss. Yes, that should do it, I thought as I give myself a once over in the hallway mirror.

As I walked across campus to the history building, I saw Stellen walking with a girl. She was very pretty but kind of slutty too. She was wearing too much black eye liner, her shirt was too low in the front, and she had a wiggle in her walk. This seemed to be his type since he broke up with me for Monika. She was like that – too sexy, if you asked me. I know I sounded like a prude but that's not me.

He saw me and started to get that nervous look. I gave him a smile and a wave and kept walking. When I got to class, I settled into my seat and opened my notebook. We were studying the assassination of Abraham Lincoln. Our professor, Mr. Blue was old-fashioned. He wore a bow tie and used words like scrumptious and whilst. He seemed like he was from another time. I noticed Francesca George and gave her a little wave. She walked over and sat by me. We both worked at the Coffee Shoppe and she was a Psychology major.

After class, we walked out together. I had wanted to ask her something for a while now. No time like the present.

"Hey, Frankie; I've got a question."

She turned to look at me. Her large red spiky curls trailing down over shoulders. She looked like a Scottish Princess.

"If a man is a big flirt and likes to hit on girls, and it's kind of a pattern, could he kill someone if they reject him?" I was thinking of Mr. Hammond.

She thought or a moment. "Sure, he could. Some people just can't handle rejection, especially if they're a sociopath or exhibit that kind of behavior. They see that as a betrayal and will automatically try to get revenge. Murder is the best revenge." She said without emotion.

"So, someone who has never killed before could just snap?" I asked.

"Yes, it happens all the time. People snap for all kinds of reasons but mostly if they feel threatened or if their loved ones are threatened. Some people, especially men snap when they are insulted. And men see rejection as an insult."

I thanked her and walked away. I checked my watch. I had a half an hour before I had to meet Caleb. I'd better hustle. As I drove to Polly's Diner, I started to think about an article I'd read in this morning's paper about our illustrious mayor.

Everett Garabedian was a transplant from New York City who moved here twenty years ago to attend college and stayed. He was a big shot at the General Electric and when that left town he decided, his new career was politics. He first ran for the City Council and was elected easily. He kept his head down and stayed there for five years and then took a job as the City Engineer helping to build the local airport.

Our old mayor got voted out after the Syrian refugee disaster. He made an agreement with the Governor's office to take in one hundred Syrian refuges without consulting with the City Council or the citizens. The opponents of this idea scared the voters by telling them the few jobs in Agatha Falls were going to the refugees. The people revolted and threw out the mayor in the next election. Garabedian ran on a campaign of job creation for the 'people of Agatha Falls'.

I'm sure that was his way of saying, not the refugees but it worked and he won the election with over 50% of the vote. Since then, he'd been trying to expand our local airport. It was currently a national airport but the plan was to make it international. The town was split on this.

The environmentalists didn't like the idea because the surrounding fifty acres that were needed for the expansion had been set aside for the preservation of the New England cotton tail rabbit, which was now an endangered species in southern Connecticut. Some endangered bunny rabbit is holding up a 25 million dollar deal. The proponents were stressing job creation and the added revenue that the international airport could bring to Agatha Falls.

The nearest international airport was in New Haven and they were thriving financially. So, it was the bunny verses big business. You could tell who was against the expansion pretty easily. Some store fronts down town had drawings of a rabbit in their windows. And some entrepreneurial person made a bundle on t-shirts and hats with the cotton tail emblem.

Ali was writing a series of articles on this topic and she was shocked and disgusted at the politics, greed, and boy's club feel to the deal making. She hated that kind of stuff but I accepted it as human nature. She was against the expansion but needed to appear neutral. Her concession to the cause was to wear a rabbit's foot on her knapsack and hang another from her car mirror. I loved rabbits too but the addition of the new airport would create over 150 jobs and bring in millions, so I was kind of on the fence.

I arrived early and purposely chose a booth in the center of the diner with a perfect view of the street. There was a huge bay window in the front of the diner that had a lovely view of the city park. At 12:35, Caleb walked in wearing faded jeans, boots, and a flannel shirt. He looked more like a cowboy than a doctor. I gave him a little wave and stood up so he could see me full length. He checked me out and smiled when he saw me and we talked for a few minutes about the warmer than usual weather this past weekend.

The waitress brought our menus and I recommended the turkey club and he said that sounded fine and ordered it with Swiss cheese and a double order of onion rings and an ice tea. I wished I could eat like that. I got a tuna on rye with Diet Coke.

Suddenly, I heard a familiar female voice.

"Excuse me dear, may I borrow your sugar bowl. There's none at my table."

"Of course, here you go," he said as he handed it to her.

"My, what a lovely watch you have. Is that a Rolex?"

"Yes, it is. It was a gift." He covered up his watch self-consciously with his other hand.

"And what is that on your wrist? That black thing?" she asked.

He shoved his shirt up his forearm and removed his watch to reveal a tattoo. It was small and looked like a number eight.

"It's a tattoo I got when I graduated from medical school. Some of the guys from my fraternity thought it was a good idea for us to all get the same tattoo. It's the infinity symbol," he explained.

"My, what muscular arms you have! Do you work out locally?"

"Yes, at the Olympus Gym on Derby Street. I go every other day on the morning before my shift." He shifted in his seat uncomfortably. His face was tinged with pink. He was actually blushing from her unwanted attention.

"Well, thank you for the sugar and I'll leave you and your friend to your lunch. Toodles!" and with that Dolores sauntered back to her table in the corner.

I called Dolores early this morning to let her in on my meeting with Dr. Travis hot-to-trot-Trott. When she heard his nick name, she had to see him for herself and came up with the plan she just carried out.

75

Our food arrived and we began to eat. After a few minutes, I took out my notebook and started asking generic questions about the state of healthcare today. He answered my questions very thoughtfully. Then I asked a few personal ones. I learned that he's from Colorado and had large family. His dad was in real estate and his brothers either were in law or have their own business. His mother restored art and had her own gallery in Boulder. He was the only doctor in the family. He went to boarding school as a kid and I could tell that he came from money. He didn't have to say it but I could tell. A world traveler and an Ivy League graduate. That means money. I changed the subject.

"I saw a movie on TV about a nurse who stole drugs from the hospital she worked at. Does that stuff really happen?" I asked.

"Well, yes, but all the pharmaceuticals are locked and only certain authorized personnel have access to them. For example, in the Emergency Department, a nurse would have to use a door code specifically issued to her by security. He or she would have to document the usage of that drug. There's a lot of paperwork for that. We also have cameras all over the hospital."

"Okay, good to know; but how about a nurse or another member of hospital staff stealing from patients? I saw that movie too." I said quickly.

"Again, we have cameras all over and we ask patients not to bring anything of value to the hospital especially if they are going to be admitted. Sometimes if the patient forgets, we lock them in a safe. Each floor has one and only security has the key."

"How do you know you can trust security?" My question hung in the air for a moment.

He looked surprised.

"Well, I guess that's up to the human resources department to hire and vet the applicants to make sure they are honest and trustworthy. He looked at his watch then. He had to go and asked for the check. He paid in cash and then walked out with me following him. I had to see his vehicle. Did he drive a yellow mustang convertible?

We got to the parking lot and he walked over to a black Corvette. He got in and waved at me. I waved back, disappointed. I walked back to Polly's Diner. Delores was waiting for me. I sat down at her table. "Well, what do you think?"

"I think he's delicious!" I just rolled my eyes.

We talked for a few more minutes and I checked my watch. It was almost 3:00. I needed to stop by the Dragon's Lair and then the Department of Motor Vehicles. They closed at 5pm. so I'd better hurry.

I walked down Main Street and cross over to Court Street, which had a gigantic Catholic Church at one end and an Episcopal Church at the other. The City Public Library sat squarely in the middle.

The Dragon's Lair was directly behind the library in a little stone building that was circa 1889. It was a historical building that had seen many businesses within its walls. Now, it was a tattoo and piercing shop. And busy too. When I walked in, I saw several people sitting and waiting. So, I browsed the walls showcasing the hundreds of tattoos available. I spotted the infinity sign almost immediately. It was a popular one.

The owner was a local boy in his late twenties who formerly was a yacht salesman but since we were an hour from the ocean and not the richest town in Connecticut, he wisely changed career plans.

There's a woman sitting at the desk. She was almost entirely covered in ink. Her arms, chest, and face had designs covering her. I walked up to her. Maybe she can help me. She looked at me. I smiled. She did not.

"Hi, I'm writing a paper for school about tattoos. Can I ask you a question?"

"You want Mick," she said pointing to the back of the store. I saw the door but it was closed.

"Is he busy?"

"He's always busy."

"Well, it will only take about ten minutes."

She exhaled loudly and slid off her stool. She was gone for almost an entire five minutes. Then she returned and waved me back toward the door.

"You can go in."

I walked in the back office. There, behind a desk sat a man with a face like a tiger with stripes and all. He smiled and revealed two fangs where his bicuspids once were. Oh my god, what have I gotten myself into?

"Hi, what can you tell me about the infinity tattoo?" I tried to act casual but it wasn't easy speaking to someone with a face like that.

"What do you want to know?" He stretched himself out in the leather chair, exposing long muscular tattooed arms as well.

"I need to know if Joey Taylor got one here back in late June or early July of this year."

"I can't tell you that, it's private."

I was ready for this. "In the state of Connecticut, a minor can only get a tattoo with their parents or guardians permission. This girl was 17 years old and did not have permission. Therefore, you broke the law and are subject to a fine up to $500.00 and six months in jail. And your shop will be closed." I said all this in one breath.

"Are you police?" he asked looking at me up and down, trying to size me up.

"No, I'm just someone who needs to know if Joey got her tattoo here. I know legally you have to keep records for seven years so show me the records."

He stood up and went to his computer and punched some keys.

"When was this?" he asked.

"It was this year, late June or early July."

He typed for a few minutes and I sat down taking in the art on the walls. Surprisingly, his taste was similar to mine. I recognized a reproduction of a Goya print I liked very much. Hmmm, I need to learn not to judge a book by its cover.

Finally, after a few minutes he said, "Here it is." He handed me a printout. She was here. July 14th. It was a Friday night. She paid cash.

"Was she alone?"

"I don't remember."

"Did she say why she was picking this particular symbol?"

He thought for a minute and then shook his head. I took the picture out of my bag. Emily gave it to me. It showed her standing under a tree and Joey is smiling.

She was wearing a denim jacket and her long brown hair was in a French braid; she looked like your typical American teen age girl. It was heartbreaking. I shoved it in his face.

"Remember this girl? She was strangled to death a month ago in the North Woods. I'm trying to find her killer." He looked at the picture and then at me.

"Yeah, I remember her now. She came alone. She got the infinity one because she said her boyfriend had the same kind. She wanted them to match."

Bingo.

I left the Dragon's Lair and headed over to the DMV. It was almost 4:30 so I didn't have much time. I pulled into the parking lot. It was vacant. I walked in and asked for Ben Hadley, I texted him after I left the shop. I sat in a very uncomfortable chair and waited. Ten minutes passed and finally he walked down the hall toward me. He gestured me into his office.

"Are you okay?" he asked.

"Why?"

"You look different. Your eyes are wild."

"Well, it's been a long day. So, what do you have for me?" I was irritated and Ben could see that.

"I have a list but first you have to promise me something." He had almost the same look on his face that Stellen got whenever he saw me. It was fear.

"Yes," I said anticipating something I'd been expecting all along.

"I want you to have dinner with me sometime."

"Okay, when?"

He looked shocked but relieved. He exhaled deeply. You know, Ben wouldn't be so bad if had some confidence. He's really not bad looking. Tall and on the skinny side but overall, he wasn't that bad.

"How about Salvatore's; it's my favorite restaurant." I suggested.

"Okay, sounds good. Now, let's talk cars. There are only two cars matching the description you gave me. One is in Litchfield and the other in Bridgeport. You said 1967 but I looked for all mustangs, which didn't make that much of a difference. There's still only two in the state. If the car isn't registered, then we won't find it this way." He handed me the computer printout.

I looked at the list. I didn't recognize any of the names or locations. Well, I knew what I'd be doing this weekend. I thanked him and left. He promised to call me soon for our date. I realized as I walked out that we were the only people still in the office. When I got outside, the sky was dark and the temperature had dropped since this afternoon. Snow was predicted in the higher elevations. The weather changed so rapidly around here. I didn't remember it ever being this erratic. I hated this time of year anyway. It got dark at 4:30.

I worked tonight so I drove straight to the Coffee Shoppe. I had fifteen minutes to spare. Francesca was at the counter when I walked in so I rushed out back to grab my apron and pin up my hair.

It was a busy night. Monday nights were usually dead but since the Dunkin Donuts was closed for renovations, we'd picked up their customers. Some of the girls from my creative writing class were sitting in the corner booth and we talked for a few minutes about the upcoming holiday break. I noticed the girls turn suddenly toward the door so I looked too.

It was Mr. Hammond and he was with a really young girl. She was wearing a Claremont College sweatshirt but that's not proof that she went there. I slept in a Yale t-shirt but I didn't go there either.

He saw me. Our eyes met. He looked genuinely surprised. I guess he didn't know I worked here. Since they're sitting in my section, I walked over and handed them menus. I told them our special of the day.

"We'll need a few moments," he said dismissing me. So, I walked away but kept an eye on him.

"Freya, you have a call, its Jake," said Francesca.

I walked out back and took the call in Rob's office, "Hi Jake."

"Yeah, Freya, I'm sorry to bother you at work but I'm still in New Haven with my crew. We went to pick up some bathroom tile and plumbing fixtures that were on special order and we had to take a detour because of an accident on the highway. We are really behind schedule. By time I get back to Agatha Falls, I'll probably just crash at Lorna's place. I didn't want you to worry about me. We haven't been seeing a lot of each other lately," he said sadly.

"Sure, that's no problem. You do have a life of your own;" I said echoing Erik's words from the other night.

"Well thanks for being so understanding about it. You usually chew my ears off," he said reminding me of all the times I've bitched him out for being late and not calling me.

"I'm going straight home after work tonight anyway," I said. "Hey, since I don't have any afternoon classes tomorrow how about we get together for dinner? I've got some errands to run after class, but I'll cook your favorite; stuffed pork chops and garlic mashed potatoes with peas and biscuits. You love that."

He laughed, "That sounds good."

I felt better too knowing that my brother and I would be spending some time together. I went back out front and saw that Mr. Hammond and his girlfriend were holding hands and looking deep into each other's eyes. I glanced over at Francesca and she just rolled her eyes as I made my way over to their table.

"Have you decided yet?" I asked as sweetly as I could.

"Yes, we'll share a plate of nachos and we'll each have raspberry lemonade."

"Okay, coming right up."

I tried my best to watch them all night but with the constant stream of customers, it was almost impossible. They left together a little after 8:30 and were still hand in hand. By time 11:00 arrived, my feet were killing me. I could tell I had a great night tip wise, so that made me happy. Francesca and I cleaned up and were out front locking the doors at 11:35.We walked to our cars. I showed her my new Escape and she loved it.

"Freya, can we go somewhere to talk? I heard something today that might relate to the article you're writing on the dead girl found in the woods. It may only be gossip but I still think you should hear it." I knew instantly it was something big. Francesca was super serious and she was not one to repeat gossip. I agreed and suggested Polly's Diner. It was close by and stayed open late.

We got in our vehicles and when we arrived at the Diner, the place was empty except for an older couple having pie and coffee. We took a booth toward the back for privacy. We both ordered coffee.

She got right down to business. "I heard something today about the murdered girl. I don't know if you've heard this but there's a rumor going around at the hospital that the girl who was killed was fooling around with a doctor who worked there. I heard it from a girl in my Advanced Biology class. She's a nursing student and works there part-time as a medical assistant. Apparently, the hospital knows and had a meeting and told everyone to zip his or her lips. They said if anyone was caught spreading any rumors about their doctors, they'd be fired. Sounds like their scared, doesn't it?"

Yes it does.

"Who's the doctor? Did she say?"

"Yeah, some doctor named Caleb? He runs the ED."

"What's the girl's name? Do you think she'll talk to me?" It's been my experience that people who gossip are often reticent to speak to someone directly instead choosing to spew their gossip indiscriminately.

"I don't know. But her name is Sarah Rush and she's a senior. Here's her number." She handed me her cell and I programed her number into my directory. We paid our bill and left.

CHAPTER ELEVEN

I woke up to the sound of my cell. It was Ali calling to tell me to look at the front page of the local section of the Beacon. After a few minutes, I got out of bed, grabbed a bathrobe, and walked out onto my front porch. It was freezing. We had a frost last night and my newspaper was covered in little crystals. I brought it into the kitchen and tossed it onto the table. I checked Jake's room, he's not there, and the bed hasn't been slept in again. At this rate, he should just move in with Lorna.

I opened the paper and looked at the local section and there it was; my article for the Sentinel. The Beacon had reprinted it. And they used my title too, *NORTH WOODS STRANGLER STILL AT LARGE*.

I called Ali back. She went to the last City Council meeting and the council agreed to the expansion of the airport. They made an offer to the owner of the fifty acres and are waiting to hear back. This was big news for the town and a surprise. Just a few days ago, it looked like the deal was not going to happen.

When I got to campus, I went straight to my psychology class. We were discussing triggers, of all things. According to today's lecture, under the right circumstance a person was capable of anything. Even a gentle, mild mannered person could kill if they were forced to defend him or herself or a loved one.

Humans were very territorial and were prone to lash out if they felt threatened. Is this caused Joey's death? If she saw something and wouldn't let it go? If she was like a dog with a bone- then that could be perceived as a threat. Whatever she saw must have been serious.

After class, I met Ali for lunch. We went to the Coffee Shoppe and as I entered, I heard applause and whistles. Some of the students were standing. It was for me. Most of them were from the Sentinel and my Psych class. Even Andy Keaton was there. Clapping and smiling. I'd never seen him smile.

"Well done," said Rob. "I suppose you want a raise now that you are a serious journalist?" He patted me on the back as I took a seat with some friends from creative writing class.

"Order whatever you want, it's on me," he said. I couldn't believe it. Rob was never generous. He was notorious for being cheap. He made his own wife pay for a postage stamp if she took one out of his desk drawer at home. I ordered a turkey club and a strawberry milkshake and got cheese fries for Ali. We celebrated over carbs and sugar.

After lunch, I drove over to the high school to see if I could talk to Nurse Janine Temple. I parked my vehicle and entered the building. The nurse's office was still down the hall from the computer lab; just like when I went here.

The nurse's office was really just a large waiting room with a couple of couches and some chairs. Various posters filled the walls about STD's, transgender acceptance and a suicide hotline number. There was a petite blond behind a desk in the corner. She looked up at me.

"Can I help you? Are you a student here?" she asked.

I introduced myself and told her I was writing for the Sentinel about the murder of Joey Taylor. She gestured to the chair beside her desk and I sat down. She was young and pretty, probably around thirty and was wearing tiny seahorse earrings.

I asked her about Joey and she answered all my questions with ease. I sensed no defensiveness. When I asked her about the split lip, she remembered right away.

"When did she get that?"

"Right before the end of the school year; here let me check my records." She typed on her computer. "It was June 7th, the week before school ended. She was working on the show Oklahoma and she said she fell or bumped her mouth, something like that."

"Did she say someone had hit her?"

"No, she didn't. Why? Where did you hear that?"

"Mr. Hammond."

She laughed. "Hammond? Don't believe anything he tells you and never be alone with him."

I got the impression that she had a bad experience with him but hadn't shared it with anyone. I needed to gain her trust I told her about my experience with him. She listened, wide eyed and serious. She kept shaking her head.

Finally, she grabbed my hand and said, "If you ask me, he's dangerous. I never told anybody this because I didn't think it would make a difference and besides, I was new here and I'm an outsider. I'm from Utah. I moved here five years ago because I wanted to live in a small town in New England. You know the covered bridges, the snow, and the foliage, stuff like that. Well, one night I stayed late to get caught up on paperwork. I didn't think anyone else was here except the janitors. I walked down the hall to use the bathroom." She paused now and took a deep breath; I could tell this was hard for her.

"I was coming out of the bathroom stall and there he was. He was standing there with this look on his face. I'll never forget it. I told him to get out, I wanted privacy and then the next thing I know, is he's grabbing me and feeling me all over like a giant octopus. He stuck his tongue in my mouth and was kissing my neck; and it was just awful. I kicked him in the groin and ran out of the bathroom. I ran back to my office, grabbed my coat and bag and ran out to my car and went home. I called in sick the next day. I didn't want to come back. But I had to, I needed my job. I had a mortgage to pay and student loans. I'm not married so I just have the one income."

We sit for a few moments not saying anything and then she continued. "That was over a year ago, when he first started here. He hasn't talked or looked at me since. It's like it never happened. I'm always debating whether or not I should tell Mr. Peabody but it's my word against him and it was last year. You know how people are when women come forward months or even years after something like that. People don't believe them. And I need my reputation for this job. I'd hate to lose that. So I keep silent. Please don't print this."

"No, of course I won't. I think you are a very brave person."

I stood up to leave. She asked me if I've ever attended the City Council meetings. They were every Monday and Thursday night. They were discussing the possibility of hiring a medium to help with the Taylor murder. Now, I was really interested.

"Whose idea was that?" I asked.

"A group of townspeople raised the money. Anyway, this medium can supposedly stand at the spot where someone died or was killed and know who did it and how it happened. She's got her own local show in Salem, Mass. That's where she's from. Joey was killed on Friday the 13th, did you realize that? Well, she thinks she can tap into the spirit world."

I'm not a follower of New Age, occult or paranormal stuff like that. I watched Ghost Hunters once in a while but that's just entertainment, right? There were a few girls on campus that were into Wicca but they kept to themselves. I was definitely going to this meeting. I wanted to meet her and interview her for my article.

"What does this medium call herself?" I asked Janine.

"Her professional name is the Salem Medium but her legal name is Nancy Johnson. Not as impressive, is it?" She asked smiling. I thanked her and left.

I had to get over to the hospital and interview the Director of the Volunteer office and get my story done by tomorrow to make my deadline And I still have to make dinner for Jake tonight.

I parked as close as I could to the front entrance. As I walked into the Volunteer Office, I noticed a very well dressed woman wearing lots of

92

jewelry sitting behind a large desk. She looked to be in her late fifties and was wearing a lot of makeup.

One window in her office was covered with plants. Spider plants, ferns, aloe, and some other plants I couldn't identify. She looked up at me finally and introduced herself as Dory Camp. I sat down in a very comfortable chair upholstered in a light blue and grey damask fabric. The walls were covered in the same matching shades.

"Hi, I'm Freya Barrett from Claremont College. I have to do a semester of volunteering and I'd like to talk to you about my working here. Is now a good time?" I asked as sweetly as I could.

While it's true that we were required to have sixty hours of volunteer work before we could graduate; there were no stipulations as to where or how it's done. Ali, for example, was volunteering at the Save the Cottontail Rabbit Foundation and Francesca was cleaning up old cemeteries. We actually had a committee in town that goes around and cleans old graves and cuts grass and brush from our two local cemeteries. St. Patrick's closed back in the 1930's but St. Bridget's was still open. The rumor around town was that St. Patrick's was haunted.

She started typing on her computer and then handed me a list. "Here is a schedule of what is available. We really need people on the 4th and 5th floor but all you young people want to work in the Emergency Department. I guess you want to be where the action is."

93

"Oh no, wherever I am needed," She smiled and I could tell she liked me.

"How soon could I start?"

"Well, you'd have to fill out this application form and you'd need one of your teachers to write you a letter of reference. Then you'd have to have a physical, to make sure you're healthy. You don't mind needles, do you?"

"Why?"

"You need to submit a blood sample as part of the medical exam."

"Oh, that's fine. I don't mind." Actually, I hated needles.

"Well, why don't we get the bloodwork and exam done today and you can drop off the paperwork to me by the end of the week. How does that sound?"

"Sure, sounds good."

We walked to the elevator. "We'll go down to the blood draw station on first floor. It won't take long."

"What's on the 4th and 5th floor? I asked.

"The 4th floor is where we keep all of our psychiatric patients. And the 5th floor has all our dementia patients," she said matter of factly. I could see why everyone wanted the ED. My choice was crazy people or demented people.

Two young men walked toward us in blue shirts wearing security badges. One looked familiar to me and then I realized he was a student at Claremont and ate at the diner sometimes. So, I waved and he walked over to me. The taller man followed him and looked at me with interest. He eyed me up and down and introduced himself as Gus, the head of security. The other man's name tag read Jon and he explained that he was being trained to cover for Gus while he was out having surgery next week. Rotator cuff- Gus told me, even though I didn't ask him.

I told Jon I was volunteering for my class credits. Gus interrupted me several times with personal questions and I became very uncomfortable. Finally, the elevator arrived and Dory and I were on our way to the lab leaving Gus behind.

We got to the lab just before closing. A young phlebotomist took my blood. It wasn't really so bad after all. Then a nurse took my blood pressure and asked me some questions. And that was it. Mrs. Camp walked with me to the front desk and shook my hand and said she looked forward to seeing me soon.

Home now, I was cooking dinner and the house smelled of fresh baked biscuits and my mom's garlic mashed potatoes. I'd left messages for Sarah Rush, the girl Francesca told me about but she hasn't contacted me yet. I'd like to speak with her personally about the rumors at the hospital. I hope she didn't get scared and refuse to talk to me. But some people were like that, they only talked through gossip.

Jake's truck roared into the driveway. He walked in with Erik, sniffed the air and said, "Fresh biscuits; they smell fantastic. Let me make a call first, I'll be right back," and he walked out of the room leaving Erik and I alone for the first time since we had dinner.

"Do you like stuffed pork chops and garlic mashed potatoes?" I asked.

"I'll eat anything," he said. He seemed tired and had shadows under his eyes.

"Are you getting enough rest?"

He shrugged. "I've got a lot going on these days. It's not anything specific. Just things," he said evasively. He helped me to finish setting the table. Jake walked back in rubbing his hands together.

"I've got to take Lorna to a concert later and then I'll probably stay over at her house. Do you mind?"

"Why don't you just marry her and then you'd be able to sleep in your own bed?"

"Marriage, are you kidding? I'm twenty-seven, give me a break."

"What concert?"

"It's at the college," he said quietly.

I thought for a moment. The only concert at
school I knew about was the Chamber Music
Ensemble doing a charity benefit for the Save the
Cotton Tail Rabbit Foundation. It was tonight. So, Jake
was going to listen to chamber music? My brother was
strictly a country music fan. He must be in love.

Over dinner, we discussed Thanksgiving and I
suggested to Jake that this year we really celebrate. We
hadn't since our parents died. I offered to cook a
turkey with all the trimmings and we could invite
Lorna over and even Dolores. Jake had never met her.
To my surprise, Jake agreed. So, I took another chance.

"Erik, would you like to come to Thanksgiving
dinner at our house?"

He thought for a moment. And just when I
thought he was going to refuse, he accepted. "Sure,
what should I bring?" he asked.

"Just bring your appetite." We finished dinner
and I took the dishes over to the sink to wash and Erik
helped me dry. Jake grabbed his coat.

"I hate to eat and run but I don't want to be
late. She gives me hell when I'm late." And with that,
he was out the door in a flash. Erik told me he was
going to be out of town for the next couple days and
was leaving Jake in charge of the renovations. After
the dishes were done, Erik left. I settled down in my
room to finish my article. I watched TV until I felt
sleepy. I soon dropped off to a dreamless sleep.

CHAPTER TWELVE

There was someone in the house. I knew it
before I opened my eyes. I heard the floor in the
hallway creak. There it was again. I slipped out of bed
as quietly as I could. I listened for more sounds but
heard nothing. I grabbed my coat, bag, and a pair of
shoes. I slipped the shoes on and slid my bag over my
shoulder so its cross-body. I opened my bedroom
window as quietly as I could and put my coat over the
sill.

I listened again. Whoever it was, they were in
Jake's office right now. I could hear drawers opening
and closing. I stuck my head out the window. It was
cold out but I stuck my head out of the window and
pushed myself through until I was about two feet from
the ground.

I let myself fall. Thank goodness, I'm on the
first floor and in the front of the house. Standing now, I
pulled my coat off the window sill and put it on and
ran across the street and hid in the bushes. I dialed 911
on my cell and waited.

I told the police where I was hiding and let
them know the intruder was still inside the house. I
asked them not to use their search lights or sirens.

Jake's truck was not in the driveway, and I was grateful that he was sleeping at Lorna's house tonight.

A few minutes passed before I saw a police car driving slowly down the hill. I stood up and waved my arms until they stopped. I approached the vehicle slowly with my hands up. There were two officers and both looked young, even to me. I gave them a quick recap. They told me to stay out of it and they'd handle everything. They parked across the street from my house and one approached the back of the house while the other approached the front.

A few minutes passed and I didn't hear anything. I almost thought the intruder got away. But then, I heard yelling. It was toward the back of the house where Jake's office was located. Then I could see a flashlight coming toward me. It was one of the officers. They've caught the guy.

"Who is it?" I asked.

"He's not carrying any ID and he's not talking. He's already lawyered up." He sounded disgusted.

"Can I see him?"

As we walked into my kitchen, I saw a tall man all in black. He had a mask pulled down around his neck and was handcuffed from behind. He turned to look at me. It was Travis Hammond.

Three hours later, sitting in the police station with Jake and Lorna, we were still waiting for an update from Deputy Carmichael. The police arrested

Hammond for breaking and entering and attempted theft. He had Jake's lap top in his duffel bag. According to the arresting office, he tried to say I had invited him over but that didn't hold up since he broke the window in our back door to get in. Now, he was threatening to sue me and the Beacon and the Sentinel for libel. Apparently, the article being printed in this morning's paper was more than he could handle. It didn't mention him by name but does say that a local high school teacher had a history of sexual harassment charges against him. It doesn't take a genius to figure out who that was.

Sheriff Hadley recused himself from the interrogation because he's Hammond's cousin. Deputy Carmichael told us we could go home and they'd let us know if they had more information for us. They're holding Hammond for 48 hours. I'm glad I left my laptop locked in my car. I'm sure that's what he was looking for when he broke in last night.

The drive home was interesting. Jake wasn't talking at all now; which meant he was probably mad at me and I'd eventually get blamed for this whole thing. We dropped Lorna off at her house and then headed home in total silence. When we pulled into the driveway, the first thing he did was cover the window in our back door with some cardboard. Then he said he was getting a security system for the house no matter what it cost. He got back in his tuck and took off.

Since I had the house to myself, I settled in the dining room getting caught up on homework assignments. A couple hours passed and the front door bell rang. I glanced out the front window and saw a black SUV parked out front. I answered the door to a middle-aged white guy in a black suit and a thirtyish white woman with a severe hair cut in a plain grey suit.

"Are you Freya Barrett?"

"Who wants to know?"

She pulled out a badge. "I'm Special Agent Margo Bent and this is Special Agent Douglas Mooney and we're from the FBI. We'd like to ask you some questions about the Joey Taylor murder. Are you Ms. Barrett?" I nodded. "May we come in?"

I let them in and I walked into the sun porch off the dining room. This was my favorite room in the house. It was the newest part too. My parents had it built a year before they died. It was my mom's plan to sit out her and knit after she retired. She never got that chance.

We were all standing. I'm not sitting until they do. I know that's part of police tactics. Whoever is standing has the upper hand so I'm not sitting. I'm not speaking either. Let them start. So, there we were standing and not talking. The seconds passed. They think that I'll speak out of nervousness or the need to fill the silence but I'm not falling for that either. Finally, the woman spoke.

"Miss Barrett, we'd like to ask you about the article you wrote for the college paper that was reprinted in the local paper this morning. I'm sure you're already aware of that." She waited. I still said nothing.

She continued, "Can you share your investigative techniques with us? We would be so grateful to learn from you." I don't like her condescending attitude. So I decided to make things difficult. I played dumb.

"What do you mean?"

"The people you spoke to, we need their names."

"Why?"

"We need to speak with them."

"Why?"

"Because we are conducting an investigation," she said wearily.

"Really, because I thought you were here to rule out the possibility of a serial killer. Do you now think the North Woods Strangler is a sequence killer? And if so, what is that based on? Originally, you believed the killings were unrelated. Has that changed?" I asked confidently.

They looked at each other but said nothing. This time, the man spoke.

"Freya, may I call you Freya?"

I nodded.

"We could really use your help here. From reading your article, you have a strong grasp on the psychology of the killer. How did you come by that?" he asked this in a friendly way. They were playing good cop bad cop now. But, I'm on to them.

I was ready for this. "According to the United States Constitution, I don't have to talk to you. I also don't have to reveal my sources either. You've heard of the constitution I presume. Do they still teach that at Quantico? If you have any questions, you can refer them to my lawyer, Richard Habermann, he's in the book. Now, if you'll excuse me, I have homework to finish." And I walked over to the front door, opened it, and waited.

At first, they just stood there, not moving. But finally, they did and as they walked by, they each handed me their business card. I took the cards without looking at them. As Agent Bent passes by, she stopped right in front of me. She was almost my height. We were eye to eye.

"This is not a game. I don't know who you think you are but we will speak to you eventually one way or the other; lawyer or no lawyer." She walked out of the house with Agent Mooney trailing her and saying nothing.

Jake arrived home a few minutes later. He immediately started installing the home security system. I swear it took us longer to agree on a password than it did to set the thing up. I called Keith and let him know about my visit from the FBI. He told me not to worry; they were just trying to intimidate me. In the meantime, he'd let Professor Rothstein know.

I told Jake nothing about my visit from the FBI. He'd freak, if he knew about that. So, I started to get ready for my dinner with Ben. He arrived on time. I knew he wasn't the type to be late. He immediately told me how lovely I looked and I almost laughed because of the big bulky parka I was wearing.

Salvatore's was a family owned and run Italian restaurant that opened back in 1959. Kind of tacky on the inside with booths lining the walls and tables in the center of the room covered in red and white checkered table cloths; it had a cozy atmosphere and made you feel like you were having a home cooked meal. I used to come here when I was a kid. My parents really liked this place. Jake and I came here occasionally but we hadn't been for a while now. I ordered the minestrone soup and Ben got fettuccini Alfredo.

We're seated at a table toward the front, which was fine because we had a lovely view of the City Park. We started to talk about how busy our lives were these days. Ben told me about his new home that he just bought. With his great aunt passing away at the beginning of last summer, he now had the money to afford a home of his own.

"Yeah, I inherited quite a bit. She was very frugal and she lived like a hermit. She was 97 when she passed."

"So, you're a descendant." I said this almost in an accusatory manner and he picked up on it right away.

"Look, I know people think that the Putnam's, Pringle's, and Hadley's have it easy because of our connection to the founder of this town but I have to get up every day and go to work like everyone else. You remember what high school was like for me. I wasn't popular and it wasn't easy."

He was right. Ben was bullied daily and he didn't deserve that. His dad was a big shot CPA at a local firm. They handled the accounts for a lot of the wealthier citizens of Agatha Falls. He threatened to sue the school of they didn't stop his son's bullying. If Ben didn't come from money, the school probably wouldn't have done anything.

The threat of a law suit forced then Principal Pelucci to resign and opened the door for Mr. Peabody to become the new principal of Evergreen High School. Since Peabody took over, the bullying had stopped, maybe not all of it but at least the teachers no longer ignored it. Unfortunately, Ben's dad died last year of a sudden heart attack and he lost his mom to cancer when he was in middle school, so his life hasn't been all sunshine and lollipops.

"I'm sorry, Ben. I didn't mean that. So, who else inherited?"

"Me, since my dad died last year. My aunt and uncle, and my great-uncle inherited the bulk of it. We're the only family she had left. Juanita never married or had kids and Uncle Linus doesn't have kids either. He divorced last year. Did you know that? And Uncle Maurice's son died years ago. So, we're it."

So, the sheriff, the town council president, and the judge inherited. Our food arrived and we ate in silence for a while. Ben explained how things are done at his job. He was nervous but eventually relaxed enough to ask about the yellow mustang.

"I'm going to Litchfield because it seems like the best lead. The owners in Bridgeport are over 70 and I don't believe their driving around Agatha Falls at night." I explained.

"So, if you find the owner, you find the killer, is that it?" He asked.

"Kind of, I mean there has to be a connection to the murder. Her sister saw the car but the police don't believe her so there not even looking into it. Someone has to follow this lead."

After Ben drove me home, I gave him a kiss on the cheek. I could tell he was disappointed but I'm not the type to lead a guy on. I told him we'd keep in touch. I checked my phone as soon as I walked in. There was a message from Sarah and she was willing to talk to me. I texted her back and we set up a time to meet.

I went right to bed. It was a long day. I didn't even watch TV or read, I was that tired. I fell asleep immediately. But, I had a dream. I'm at the falls and just about to cross the river, as I did when I was a kid.

But as I'm crossing, someone starts following me. So, I speed up and when I do, I slip. As I start to go over the side, someone grabs me from behind but when I turn around to face them, I wake up. I never saw their face.

CHAPTER THIRTEEN

The council met tonight. I switched shifts with Bonnie at the Coffee Shoppe so I could go. The Beacon reported this morning that the council's agenda would include the hiring of the Salem Medium. The town is divided over it. Some thought it was great idea, while others thought it was a waste of money. I had the chance to look this morning on You Tube. There she was, the Salem Medium, she was a pretty blond in her thirties and a single mom, not at all, what I expected.

As I'm leaving the diner, I checked my watch, I had enough time to stop home and change and grab a bite to eat before the meeting. As I approached my vehicle, I noticed a package on the hood of my vehicle.

There was a white box and it stood out against the red of my hood. I looked around but didn't see anyone. I had parked in the far corner of the lot, where I always park. What should I do? I have this image of an explosion and I'm being blown to smithereens.

The package was small, about 10x10 inches. I slid the box over to the edge of the hood, took it very gently, and laid it on the ground. I got in my car, drove over, and parked on the opposite side of the street. I called the police and asked for Deputy Carmichael. Thankfully, he's on duty. I quickly explained the situation and he listened to me with interrupting.

"Stay where you are. Don't touch it. I'll be there in ten minutes."

I went back inside the diner. There were only a couple of customers and just Rob and Bonnie behind the counter. I told Rob that the police were coming because a suspicious looking package was in the parking lot. He didn't ask any questions, and told his customers and Bonnie they needed to leave the diner now.

"I'll explain everything once we are across the street, let's go," he told them.

By time we exited the building, the police had arrived with a van and two other police cars. One officer was putting up police tape and another was setting up orange cones in the road. Once the area was cordoned off, the side door to the van opened and a drone the size of a back pack rolled down the ramp. Deputy Carmichael explained that the drone would try to examine the package and detonate it, if it turned out to be a bomb.

By now, a small crowd of people assembled to watch. The drone rolled itself over to the package and stopped. An officer inside the van was operating it. There was a camera on the drone so the officer could see what it saw.

The drone began squirting water at the package. Carmichael explained that if it was a bomb, the water would activate the wires causing it to detonate on site. We waited. Nothing happened. The drone extended an arm like extension and began ripping open the package. It pulled out some tissue paper.

We were too far away to see anything. But suddenly, Carmichael's walkie-talkie went off. It was loud enough for us to hear the officer saying the package appeared harmless. The drone rolled over to the van and the officer took the tissue paper from its arm. Carmichael ran over. For a few seconds he studied what the office handed him. He then walked over to me to show me the find.

It was a girls' size ring, silver with a peridot stone in its center. Joey. It must be hers. I told the Deputy this but he just looked at it and said nothing for a moment.

"We'll send it to the lab. Don't write about this please. We already look like a bunch of idiots." He looked tired. My cell went off. It was Dolores.

"Hey, what's up?"

"Guess what I just heard?" she asked excitedly.

"What?"

"The FBI searched Joey's phone and found over three dozen calls made between her and Trott last summer."

110

"What about texts?"

"They're still reviewing them. I'll let you know if I hear more."

I hung up and drove over to the Taylor residence. I needed to know if Joey owned a peridot ring. The Subaru was in the driveway and I saw Emily in the front window. She smiled and gave me a huge wave. She opened the door before I have a chance to knock. When I walked in, most of their belongings had been packed up in boxes.

"We're moving to Ohio next weekend. That means I won't see you anymore." She looked so sad.

"We can Skype." She looked up hopefully when I said this.

"Emily, did Joey have a peridot ring? Silver and small like a pinky ring?"

"My mom got her that for Christmas last year."

"Where is your mom?"

"Sleeping, what else is new? But I rather have that than her crying all day."

"So, you're all alone?"

She nods. I looked at my watch. It was 5:30, enough time to get something to eat before the meeting.

111

"Hey, how would you like to get some dinner with me tonight? Have you eaten today?"

"I had a pop tart this morning."

"Well, grab your coat, you're coming with me."

Suddenly excited, she ran out back and was gone for a few minutes. When she returned she had her jacket and told me, she left her mom a note, just in case. A half hour later, we were eating BLT's and sharing French fries at Polly's Diner. She told me all about her school and her cousins in Ohio. After we finished we walked back to my car and she told me that the FBI stopped the other night to talk to her and her mom. She didn't like them. I didn't say anything. They asked questions about Joey's job at the hospital and Mr. Hammond. Her mom didn't know much and neither did she, so they left. How interesting, I thought. What does the FBI know?

I dropped her off and told her to call me if she needed anything. She hugged me and I wondered if this is what it felt like to have a little sister. I drove to City Hall and it was packed. I almost couldn't find a space to park.

The Channel 5 news was there and a couple of reporters from the Beacon. I arrived with five minutes to spare. I took a seat toward the back of the room. The council meetings were held in the basement of the City Hall. The room held about a hundred people and it was almost filled to capacity. The council took roll call and then got right down to business. The secretary read the minutes from last week. The mayor spoke.

"We will begin the meeting tonight regarding the hiring of a medium to pursue the recent murder of a local teen age girl. The police in Massachusetts have used Ms. Johnson and find her to be highly credible. She has been responsible for solving many cold cases and has a popular local cable access show in Salem. I'd like to begin the voting, if no one here has anything to say?"

"Yes, I have something to say." A well-dress older woman walked up to the podium.

"I would like to know how much this medium is going to cost the tax payers of this town. I'd also like to know why we, the voters don't have a say about what happens here?" The room erupted in clapping and cheering.

Mayor Garabedian looked at Juanita Hadley and she nodded her head. He took the microphone and stood up. "The cost of Ms. Johnson's professional reading is being paid for by a group of citizens who donated the money. No tax payer dollars are being used for her services." He sat down to a smattering of applause from the audience. He looked very satisfied with himself.

An older man approached the podium. I recognized him. It was Quentin Ambrose, the local environmentalist and leader of the Save the Cottontail Rabbit Committee. He's spoken at my college about

113

many environmental and human rights issues. I liked him.

"Good evening, Honorable Mayor, distinguished members if the City Council, and Ms. Hadley. Thank you for taking my question. To start, I don't have an issue with concerned citizens hiring a medium to help solve the murder of Joey Taylor; hell, I'll pay for it myself if I think it will find the monster that killed that child."

"But what I do have an issue with is greed, back-room deals and collusion." Total silence- you could hear a pin drop.

"I know for a fact that you, Ms. Hadley will benefit financially from the airport expansion. And you, honorable mayor will also make a pretty penny."

By this time, the room had erupted in voices and loud talking and all eyes were riveted to the speaker and the mayor.

"This is slander and I won't stand for it." The mayor said while he stood up and walked over to the podium facing the speaker.

"I don't care what you stand for but you will let me finish what I came here to say," said Ambrose to a round of applause from the audience who was clearly on his side.

"Since Eloise Putnam-Pringle's death, Sheriff Hadley, Juanita Hadley, and Judge Pringle have become direct beneficiaries of her massive estate," he said.

"Miss Eloise owned the fifty acres that lie adjacent to our current airport and was dead-set against the expansion since it would destroy the habitat of the New England cottontail rabbit."

"But now that she is dead, the land reverts to you, Ms. Hadley, and your brother the sheriff. I say today, that you are in collusion with the mayor to expand this airport and will personally gain financially from this dirty deal."

"Collusion is not illegal," said the mayor, directing his response to the crowd. He returned to the podium and grabbed the gavel in his hand banged it loudly. "Now, if anyone else has a question. We need to move on."

"No, the act of collusion is not illegal in itself, but it leads to illegal and unethical acts," responded Quentin to thundering applause from the audience, ignoring the mayors attempt to change the subject.

The gavel was heard through the voices of the crowd and he spoke again, "The statements made this evening against myself, Ms. Hadley, Sheriff Hadley and the Honorable Judge Pringle are slanderous."

"And if the Beacon prints any of it, I will sue for libel. These statements have no merit. A delusional and sick person who has their own agenda is making them. This meeting is adjourned."

He banged his gavel one final time and stood to leave and Juanita Hadley followed behind leaving the remaining seven members of the council sitting there not knowing what to do. Eventually, they stood and walked out slowly, not speaking to the local media who was following them out the door. What a scene.

I made my way over to Quentin. Surrounded by a crowd, he was being interviewed by Les Murray from the Beacon. Les was a former writer for the Washington Post and had retained his quarterback physique from college days. He shoved a few people away as they tried to interrupt his interview with Quentin.

"One at a time," he snapped. Les was not known for his personality but more for his tenacity and writing skill. A former nominee for the Pulitzer, he wasn't afraid to play David to fight Goliath. I respected him.

He saw me, "Hey, Freya, you want to ask some questions next?"

I nodded and smiled. He walked Quentin and me over to an alcove in the corner of the meeting hall and I introduced myself and started to ask questions, taking notes at the same time. Quentin told me how much he liked my articles about Joey and agreed to meet with me for a lengthier interview. He gave me directions to his home and we set a time for tomorrow. He lived on the outskirts of town on the older north side by the woods.

It was late so I left for home. As I neared my house, I saw Jake waiting for me at the back door.

"I've got news for you."

"What?" I'm tired and just want to go to sleep. It's been a long day.

"Deputy Carmichael just called. The police searched Hammond's house and personal and work computer. Guess what they found?"

"I don't know- what?"

"Child pornography, thousands of pictures and – get this- pictures of Joey, undressed."

"Did she pose for him? I don't believe it." I'm actually shocked at this. I knew he had a problem with young girls but I didn't see this coming.

"No, the cops found a hole in the girl's locker room. That pervert has been filming the girls in the locker room and girl's bathroom. He's been arrested. Carmichael called as a favor to us, to let us know he wouldn't bother us anymore. It'll be in the paper tomorrow. He just wanted to give us a heads up."

Jake walked into the living room and turned on the TV. I could tell he was happy with the news. Just then, the phone rang. It was Dolores. Before I could even say hello, she was talking.

"The shit has really hit the fan down here," she said almost out of breath. "Hammond tried to hang

117

himself in his jail cell tonight; he's in the ICU at Mercy Regional in critical condition. They don't know if he's going to make it. He's unresponsive. And get this, he used his shoelaces; the cops never took his shoes away so they're culpable now."

"Earlier today, they found a load of dirty pictures on his computers and apparently he's been watching the girls at the high school and filming them without their consent. And get this; the feds want Hadley to step down as sheriff and Carmichael to take his place. The mayor even agreed to it."

I stopped her for a second. It was too much information to take in all at once. I told her about my afternoon with the bomb squad.

"Oh my God, I wondered what that was all about. Are you all right? I heard about something happening over at the Coffee Shoppe."

"Yeah, I'm fine. But why would someone send me Joey's ring?"

"I don't know. But I'll check to see if the lab has a report on it yet. Look, I've got to go. The FBI is in a meeting right now with Carmichael and the mayor. What a night. "

Yes, I agreed, what a night. I went to bed and fell asleep almost instantly but I dreamed again.

I dreamed I was locked in a room full of smoke and I couldn't get out. I started screaming, but no one could hear me. I finally woke up drenched in sweat. It was 3:00. I went into the kitchen for a glass of water and as I passed by the front window, I saw a car parked out front of my house. The driver must have seen me because it drove off fast. I opened the front door and walked out onto the cold night air, but I was too late. The car was gone.

CHAPTER FOURTEEN

The front page of the paper was devoted to the recent promotion of Deputy Carmichael to the position of sheriff. It gave his biography as if he were new to the area and not a local boy who was born here, attended school here and lived here his whole life. It mentioned that Sheriff Linus Hadley had taken an early retirement but didn't say anything else. The rest of the paper was devoted to Mr. Hammond's porn and voyeur fetishes. I was so engrossed in the paper that I was almost late for class. Thankfully, there was no mention of the suspicious package or the drone.

When I arrived on campus, I headed right to Professor Rothstein's office. She was on the phone so I took a seat and waited. Her office was very plain. No personal photos or pastel colors for her. All I saw was the color grey and file cabinets.

She hung up and I quickly gave her a recap as to yesterday's events: the package, the council meeting, the medium, and my volunteering at the hospital. She sat back in her seat and raised one eyebrow. "Well, no one will ever call you lazy."

"Would you write me a letter of reference for my hospital volunteer job?"

"Of course, I'll have it for you by this afternoon, is that okay?"

"Sure, my last class ends at 2pm. I can come back after that."

"Freya, be careful." She looked at me over her coffee mug. Her expression was deadly serious.

I met Ali and Lincoln on the way to class and filled them in on the council meeting the night before. I got an idea.

"Hey what are you doing later?"

"After class, I'm going home, why?"

I explained about my meeting with Quentin and asked her if she'd like to come with me. She did so we planned to meet after my last class at the Coffee Shoppe. I reached my English Literature class with five minutes to spare.

We were discussing the theme of fate in Macbeth. Our assignment was to write 3,000 words on whether we believed Macbeth's fate was determined by destiny or free will. I wrote that his actions suggested that fate may be predetermined but his free will determined his destiny.

I saw a lot of parallels between Macbeth and Agatha Falls. For example, one theme of the play was that unchecked ambition was a corrupting power. Between the mayor, the former sheriff, and the City Council, I saw a lot of corruption. I was starting to think that was really, what got Joey killed. Now, I just had to prove it.

After my class ended, I rushed over to Rothstein's office. Her secretary had the letter for me and then I ran, literally across the quad to reach the Coffee Shoppe. Ali was engrossed in conversation with Rob.

"You never said anything about the bomb squad." She was irked at me for not telling her and I'm pissed at Rob for telling her – what a mess.

"It wasn't a bomb squad, it was a little drone. And besides, I'll tell you everything. Come on, or we'll be late." I knew her well enough to know she felt left out but I had to be careful about what I shared with her. She was my best friend but I hadn't shared that much with her about my investigation. She frowned on my methods and would think them unethical and dangerous. We walked out to the car and as I drove, I explained about the package and the ring. I told her the basics, nothing too specific.

"So, it was probably left for me because I wrote the story, that's all. I'm not worried about it." If she believed, there was more to it than that she didn't say, but she's smart. I left it there and changed the subject to my upcoming volunteering job at the hospital.

I needed to stop at Mercy Regional and drop my paperwork off. As I approached the Volunteer Office, Agent Margo Bent was there speaking with Dory so I hid behind a laundry cart before she could see me. I waited a few minutes, but Bent was still there. I ended up leaving the envelope with the woman sitting at the front desk. She promised me that Dory would get it.

There must be a connection between Joey's murder and the hospital if the FBI was interviewing the head of the volunteers. I shared nothing of this with Ali as I drove. Quentin's house was on the outskirts of Agatha Falls and we had to cross the covered bridge to get there.

Hawthorne Bridge as it was called in the 1800's was once owned by Samuel Hawthorne, no relation to Nathaniel Hawthorne, until his family sold it in the 1930's. Now, the state of Connecticut owned it and it was a historical site. It was well preserved and one of the highlights of our little town. As we passed through the bridge, we come to a private road that reads - *trespassers will be violated.*

Thankfully, the road was paved and we drove for almost ten minutes until the house was before us. A lovely Gingerbread Victorian; it was white with light blue and green trim and wraparound porch. The front yard was surrounded by a perennial garden now gone by for the season. A brass cupola adorned the roof and there was an image of a lion engraved on it. It was very impressive

"I love this house," exclaimed Ali. "I can't wait to see the inside."

Quentin lived alone since his wife passed last year from cancer. His children were grown and lived in

North Carolina. He mentioned plans about retiring there someday but hated giving up his home.

We walked up the porch stairs and knocked at the door. The brass knocker was in the shape of a lion too. Quentin must have a thing for lions. St. Patrick's cemetery was to the left of us at the bottom of a big hill that ran adjacent to the house. Supposedly haunted, it was closed now, but it still got visited by the local historical club and an occasional ghost hunter. Every Halloween and Friday the 13th, cemetery tours were scheduled. Apparently, they were so popular there was a waiting list.

I knocked again and waited. It was after 3pm. Did he forget? Ali and I walked around back. Maybe he was in the garden. The back yard was bordered by the Old North Woods in the back and a large lily pond on the right. It was beautiful out here. A large white marble fountain sat in in the center of the yard with an angel in the middle. I had no idea his property was so elaborate. We started walking down a little trail that led into the woods. A wrought iron fence bordered the yard. Seeing something on the ground, I went closer to get a better look. That's when I saw it.

Scattered about the walkway, there was a man's boot, a ripped shirt and a set of keys. Then, farther down the way, a sock and then a pair of pants were just lying on the ground. What's going on? Is he a nudist? It's 45 degrees out; he'd have to be crazy.

We kept walking and then noticed something farther ahead. It was a pit or a big hole in the ground, freshly dug. A shovel was beside it on the ground.

I looked over to the edge and peered inside. I gasped. My hand went to my mouth as it always did when I'm shocked or upset. Ali came toward me but I pushed her away.

"Don't look." That was all I said. She stood there with a scared look on her face. I peered back down into the hole, saw a man's body, naked, and face down in the dirt. Something was not right and that's when I realized he had no head. His body was deathly white. I didn't see any wounds other than the obvious one and there was no blood.

I backed away grabbed Ali's hand, led her back to the front porch, and called 911. I explained what I'd found and gave my name. I could just imagine what the FBI would think now, between the suspicious package, the break in and now this. We sat and waited in silence. Twenty minutes passed before we heard the police car sirens. Why they're using that, I don't know. It's too late to save him now.

It was like watching an episode of CSI. We watched for a while until a detective I'd never seen before took my statement and then Ali's. After an hour, he told us we could leave. As we were driving down the private road, a familiar black SUV was driving toward the house, the FBI. I'm so glad we left when we did.

As we were driving home, Ali turned to me breaking the silence said, "Where's the head?" That's a good question. I don't know but there was one thing I do know. Quentin was murdered by the same person who killed Joey. All I had to do was prove it.

125

CHAPTER FIFTEEN

As we drove over the covered bridge on our way back into town, I invited Ali to the medium's reading in the woods that evening.

"I'm still going tonight to the psychic reading in the woods. Do you want to come with me? Maybe, Lincoln and Francesca will come too. What do you think?"

I knew from experience that Ali wasn't interested in anything supernatural. Some of our friends were into Wicca. I was raised a Catholic, although I don't go to church anymore, I still consider myself a Catholic. Ali was Presbyterian and I don't really know anything about that faith. But Ali did go to church once a week with her dad and she was not a fan of horror movies either. I wasn't sure if she wanted to see the medium. But I asked anyway.

"Yes, I'll be there," she said. "I'd like to see her in person. And I'll ask Linc if he wants to come along." She was quiet and probably still in shock since finding the dead body. I wasn't feeling that well either. I just wanted to go home and lie down.

I dropped Ali off at her house and drove directly home. I texted Francesca and asked her to text me back. Then, I took a hot shower. There's a note taped to the refrigerator door from Jake. He was taking Lorna to a restaurant in New Haven and would probably crash at her place tonight. I settled down on the couch and watched some TV. At 6:30, I turned on the local news.

I loved channel 5; they did an awesome job covering the murder. Right now, they were airing a special report on the murder of Quentin Ambrose. They didn't mention my name, thankfully. The reporter was a young woman with dark framed glasses. She looked very serious.

"The coroner's office is reporting that the head was removed after death and the police have informed us that the head was located this evening on a seemingly unrelated grave in St. Patricks' Cemetery that borders on the property. The FBI is working with local police to rule out a possible connection with the October 13th murder of Joey Taylor."

"Later this evening, medium, Nancy Johnson known as the Salem Medium will do a reading in the Old North Woods in an attempt to seek answers in the murder of Ms. Taylor. Ms. Johnson has helped in other cold cases and has a high success rate; back to you, Jim."

Who said life in a small town was boring? Just then, my phone rang. It was Francesca telling me she'd meet me at the woods for the reading. I texted Ali to give her a heads up and left for the woods. When I got there, cars were everywhere and the local TV station too. It was a media circus.

127

There was a large white tent off to the side where I presumed resided the medium. Someone was even selling t-shirts that read, *I Survived the Old North Woods*. Woody Sawyer from the Beacon was interviewing people so I ran over to speak with him.

"Hey Woody, learn anything new since yesterday?"

"Nope, the cops and the Feds are quiet. That means they know something but they're not sharing it with us. Stay tuned," He said with a wink as he walked off in pursuit of another subject.

By this time, it was dark. My friends and I stood together and waited. Someone was walking around handing out candles so we each took one. There were some flood lights near the tent and the TV news crew had some overhead lights on. Beside the full moon, it was dark and the moment felt surreal.

A man emerged from the tent. He introduced himself as Ms. Johnson's assistant. He was young and had a goatee and wire rimmed glasses. He looked like a professor. He explained what was going to happen.

"Good evening. My name is Wiley Cooper and I work with Ms. Johnson. I'm a parapsychologist and have spent the last eleven years studying phenomena. There are many things in this world that are unexplainable but that doesn't mean they are all paranormal. That's why I'm here; I'm here to debunk those theories. However, it is my belief that some psychics and some mediums are the real thing. I have worked with Ms. Johnson for the past two years and I find her highly credible. You are all entitled to your own opinion but that is mine."

"On her behalf, I ask that during the reading you remain quiet and there be no flash photography. We take this seriously and ask that you do as well. Please respect the dead and respect their wishes to communicate with the living."

"We believe that death is merely another realm, and just because we cannot see it, does not mean it doesn't exist. And now I present to you, Ms. Nancy Johnson, the Salem Medium."

A young woman emerged from the tent. She was tall, blond, and slim. She had an ethereal glow about her and was dressed all in white. She reminded me of a fairy princess. All that was missing were the wings. She walked directly to the site where Joey's body was found and stood there. She turned to face the crowd but remained silent. Finally she spoke.

"Good evening. My name is Nancy Johnson. You may know me as the Salem Medium. I have always had strong intuitive abilities. I first discovered this when I was a child. Some people call what I have a gift. I don't see it that way. I've always believed that my gift is the ability to give the living a message from their loved one who has passed over. It is a gift to the living. I believe this ability is God given and in no way satanic."

"Everyone is intuitive to an extent; some more than others. I have used my ability for the last fifteen years to help reunite the living with the dead and sometimes to bring justice to those who left us too soon. Tonight I will try to reach the spirit of Joey Grace Taylor, who was murdered on October 13th; a little over a month ago." "I asked her mother to be here tonight but she has declined. I understand that some of her friends are here and I welcome that. And so does Joey. The dead are often lonely and desire communication with the living, especially those closest to them."

"Before I begin, I'd like to say one more thing. I am both a psychic and a medium. A psychic is someone who can tune in to the energy field or aura of a living person but a medium can read a person no longer in the physical body. As a medium, I am able to reach spirits who have crossed over and those that are earth bound. We know these souls as ghosts."

"Death is not the end of life; it is a transition from the living body to the spirit world. Your body is a shell. Your soul, your essence, and your own unique life force; are what make you who you are. That is the part of Joey; I will try to connect with tonight."

We were standing in a grove of balsam trees. The Old North Woods were full of them. Their fragrance was ironically comforting and reminded me of happier days. I read somewhere that balsam was the symbol of life and eternity. How twisted that Joey would die underneath them.

The medium began speaking in a low voice at first but then her voice rose so all could hear.

"Hello Joey, my name is Nancy and I'd like to speak with you tonight. Many of your friends are here. We want to know what happened to you and who did this to you. Can you tell us?"

She closed her eye and concentrated. Some of the candles flickered and then all at once, they went out. Gasps were heard from the crowd and then the low murmuring of voices. The medium spoke again.

"Joey, tell me who hurt you? Do you know this person?" The questions were asked in the same way one might talk to the living. There was no sense of anxiety. She seemed calm and relaxed. The wind had picked up and the trees were blowing with more force than before. A few small branches fell to the ground.

"Joey was killed by someone she trusted. He took advantage of that trust. She was strangled right where I'm standing. The killer wore leather gloves. I'm hearing the name Lukas now. Does that mean anything to anyone?" She asked the crowd. I looked around and saw heads shaking.

"She's s saying that someone named Caleb lied to her. I'm hearing the name Caleb now. Does anyone know this name?"

I knew that name.

"What about the car Joey? What do you want us to know?" She waited and then surprised me by what she said next.

131

"I'm seeing Joey in yellow car, it's small and old- no- not old but vintage. And the driver is yelling at her. It's a man. I can't see his face." Oh My God, the yellow mustang. I looked over to where the police were standing. I wondered what they thought now.

"Joey, who did this to you, was it the man named Lukas? I'm seeing the name Lukas and I'm seeing you here in this forest."

The wind was stronger now and the trees were rustling around us. One of the floodlights started to flicker. I had goosebumps. Ali looked like she was in a trance. Lincoln looked like he was about to faint. I was kind of in the middle myself.

The medium started to walk toward a wild barberry shrub. She looked into the crowd. "I'm getting someone else now. This sometimes happens. When the dead find out there's a medium around, they all want to talk. Don't be alarmed," she told the crowd who was visibly shaken at this point.

"Is there a Jake here?" I looked around at the mention of my brother's name. But the men in the crowd shook their heads. "Okay, what about a Freya? Is there someone here named Freya? Your mother has a message for you."

I inhaled quickly. I never expected this. Ali grabbed my arm, "Freya, it's your mom."

The medium walked over to me, "Are you Freya?" I nodded. She took my hand and held it firmly in hers.

"You are in grave danger and must act with prudence." She said in a whisper only I could hear.

"You are to act with caution and be very careful whom you trust. There is a man who wants to hurt you. He presents himself in a false light. Do not be seduced by this. He is very clever and is very charming. Your mother is with you at all times and can only protect you so much." I wasn't sure how to take this so I just stood there saying nothing.

"Your mother says to find the necklace and you will find this man."

"Is the man who killed Joey the same man who wants to hurt me?" I asked finally finding my voice.

"Yes."

"Have I already met this man?"

"Yes, I believe you have. I know that your mother is with Joey and is helping her on the other side."

"Sometimes, when a young person passes over traumatically, an older spirit will act as a guide or mentor."

I smiled. That sounded like my mother. I had so many questions but now wasn't the time to ask them.

"What should I do? Ask her." I pleaded.

"Rita-your mother is Rita? She was killed in an auto accident. No, she was killed by a drunk driver."

"Yes." Oh my God, how could she know that?

"She wants me to tell you that you already possess all the skills and qualities necessary to find this man but you must do so prudently. You must not be afraid to ask for help. You like to do things on your own but you must learn to work with others. There is an older woman, someone in law enforcement. You must trust her and give her a chance." She let go of my hand and walked away from me. She went back to the place she stood before and spoke to Joey again.

"I'm seeing a necklace. It's a locket. It was taken from this young woman. The killer took this from her and she wants it returned."

"Another man gave her this necklace and she realizes now that he loved her very much. But Joey loved another. She regrets that now. Joey, we will do everything we can to find this necklace and the man who hurt you. Peace to you."

"She's gone. I need to speak with the police."

She returned to her tent with Sheriff Carmichael following. Her assistant walked over and told the crowd that the reading had ended and thanked us for the respect we had shown.

"Ali, wait here, I'll be back in a few minutes."

134

I approached the tent but stood there not sure of how to announce myself, so I said knock-knock.

"Come in Freya."

I pulled back the curtain and looked inside. She was sitting on a chair holding a cell phone and drinking a Diet Pepsi. Sheriff Carmichael was just leaving and gave me a little nod as he exited the tent.

"I have to call my mother. She's watching my daughters," she said with a smile. I waited until she was done with her call. She seemed even younger in person.

"Freya, your parents love you very much and are proud of you. They are still with you. You are not alone. None of us are."

"Thanks, but that's not why I'm here."

I quickly explained what I needed from her and she thought for a few moments and agreed. I went in search of my friends and told them my plan. They were game. So, we went back to the tent, I pulled back the flap. The medium was waiting.

CHAPTER SIXTEEN

"Are you sure you don't mind?" I asked her again. But she still said yes. I asked her if she would do a reading pro bono at Quentin Ambrose's house. After I explained what had happened in the past two days and how it might affect Joey's murder, she agreed immediately.

"Yes, of course I'll help you. And please, call me Nancy."

My plan was to drive out there with Nancy; Ali and Lincoln wanted to follow along but Francesca begged off, she had enough excitement for one day. In spite of what I had in mind, I felt excited and emboldened. After all, according to her earlier contact with the spirits of Joey and my mom, I already possessed all the qualities and skills necessary to catch this person.

On the drive to Quentin's, I used the opportunity to ask Nancy some questions. She was very calm and answered everything I asked her. She told me she received her information in pieces and it didn't always make sense at the time. In the spirit world, there was no concept of time, as we knew it in the living world. Spirits had no idea how long they had been gone and sometimes were quite attached to their material goods and did not choose to pass over. She believed that Quentin might be easier to contact because he was older and more recently departed.

"Freya, you have a powerful aura, its red. That means that you are brave and a great leader but you must learn prudence. This killer has killed before and he doesn't have a conscious the way most people do."

"He's not a sociopath or psychotic, but he is the type of person who puts himself first and justifies his deeds because they give him what he wants. He's a selfish person and may not be acting alone. He also has shown premeditation so that means he is smart and has probably done this before."

This made me think. I often thought from the beginning that the killer was a part of something big-so maybe I was right.

The medium began speaking in a low voice. I glanced over at her. Her eyes were closed.

"I see Joey in a hallway with white walls; I think it's a hospital or nursing home. I see a pillow and beds. I see elevators and a handsome man."

"Is Lukas the killer? What about Caleb? She was dating him."

"I'm hearing the words liar with the name Caleb. You see, it's like a dream. I see images and they are random. I'm not getting them in any kind of coherent order. It's like watching a movie and the scenes are all mixed up. That's how it works for me."

How interesting. I could rarely if ever remember my dreams and when I did, they were only images. I told her this and described some of them to her.

"These are warnings," she said excitedly. "You must listen to them. Sometimes our dreams tell us of what may be. These are premonitions or intuitive dreams. Again, be prudent and act with caution. You are sensitive. I picked up on it when I met you. Use this to your advantage. Don't ignore these warnings," she urged me.

We arrived at Quentin's house. The nighttime darkness added to the eeriness. Only the yellow police tape was a reminder of what occurred that morning. Ali and Lincoln got out of her car with flashlights. I smiled. She was just like me; we always had a flashlight in our bags. We walked out back to the pit but stood a few feet back from it. The medium walked right to the edge and closed her eyes.

"This victim did not know his killer. He was waiting here for him. He came through the woods, on foot. He dug the pit and waited for the victim to walk outside to see it up close. That's when he got him."

She walked down the trail leading toward the Old North Woods and stood there.

"He was knocked unconscious here, partially undressed and dragged back up the embankment." She stands in front of the fountain. "He was killed here. He was garroted with a piece of piano wire and his head was removed here. The killer used a piece of tarp, that's why there was no blood. I need to go to the cemetery to see where the head was left."

She walked down the hill leading to St. Patrick's Cemetery and began to walk ahead of me without the aid of a flashlight. I tried to lead the way with my flashlight, but she didn't seem to need me. This cemetery was supposedly haunted and sometimes the cries of young children could be heard. I listened but the only thing I heard was my beating heart. Soon, she stopped at a head stone.

"Can you shine the flashlight here?" We read the stone. The inscription was very old, but the date was clear enough to read – 1929. The name had been worn away by weather and erosion. If the killer was trying to tell us something, we didn't know what it was just yet. I'd have to find out who was buried in this grave.

"I'm seeing a fire; but nothing more. This spirit passed over long ago. It was a male and he was killed in a fire; that's all I see. I'm not getting any messages here. I'm sorry, sometimes that happens. I'm quite tired. Freya, can you drive me back to the hotel now? It's been a long night."

"Of course, I will." I said goodbye to my friends and walked with Nancy back to the car. We drove in silence and just as I was parking in front of the hotel, I couldn't resist.

"Is this hotel really haunted? I've heard stories since I moved here about ghosts living in the hotel. Is that true?"

She looked at me as with the same serene expression she had when I met her. "Oh yes. My room is inhabited by the spirit of a Union colonel named William. He's very polite but lonely," she said sadly. "He misses his wife Eleanor. They spent their honeymoon here at the Regency. That's why he refuses to leave. Good night," she said and she walked into the hotel.

CHAPTER SEVENTEEN

My meeting with Sarah Rush was today at her residence hall on campus. Her roommate left town to visit family over the holiday so it'll be just the two of us. I wanted to speak with her before I began my volunteering next week. If there were rumors floating around about the hospital, I need to know that now. After meeting with Sarah, I planned on driving to Litchfield later today to look up the yellow mustang on my list from the DMV.

My article was in this morning's paper. The title, COLLUSION IN A SMALL TOWN was the lead story on the front page of the local section. That should shake things up around here.

Dolores called me early this morning to tell me that the ring left for me was in fact Joey's; her mom confirmed that. Unfortunately, there was no DNA found. And the list of texts from Joey's phone hadn't led to any new information either. The texts were mostly between her and her high school friends. There was nothing incriminating found.

Before meeting with Sarah, I dropped by Keith's office. We were discussing a weekly series focusing on small town crime. I was very excited about this new opportunity. As I arrived at campus, most of the parking lot was empty. Then I remembered, this was Thanksgiving week and most of the students had already left to go home to be with family. The remaining students were local kids or the ones who couldn't afford to travel.

Keith was at his desk and smiled when he saw me. This surprised me. He was not known to smile very often. "Guess who I spoke to yesterday?" he asked me. I'm not sure what to say to this so I just say I don't have any idea.

"Margo Bent."

"What did she want?" I asked this already knowing the answer. They wanted our sources.

"I didn't speak with her. I referred her to Professor Rothstein. She was in her office for about five minutes and then she left looking very unhappy."

"What did she tell her?"

"Knowing her, she probably told her to go to hell. Look, don't worry, we haven't done anything illegal, and the FBI knows it."

We spent the next half an hour going over his expectations for my weekly series. Keith had the same mind I do. We both believed that if you dig deep enough into any small town, you'll find lots of dirt. He wanted me to focus right now on some local crimes in Connecticut. Some of them were cold cases but he believed we were on to something here.

I walked over to Woodbury House from Keith's office. Most of the students here were in the nursing program. When I walked in, there was a skeleton hanging from the ceiling and it was wearing a pilgrim hat. Sarah's room was on the third floor but I walked up, foregoing the elevator. Her door was decorated for the holiday with a Thomas Kincaide foliage scene. I knocked and a dark haired girl answered. I introduced myself and she let me in.

Somebody liked Hello Kitty. The room was pink and had a Hello Kitty quilt on the bed with matching pillow cases. Sarah herself was wearing a t-shirt with the same emblem and her slippers were Hello Kitty. We sat on her bed and I asked her about the rumors she's heard. She was obviously a big gossip.

"Well, it's all over the hospital. Joey was easy. She threw herself at every man there." She explained this to me this as if we were discussing the weather and not a murdered teen ager. This girl wanted to be a nurse. Where was her compassion?

"Did you know her personally?" I asked.

"No, I'm just repeating what I've heard. Ask any of the volunteers, they'll tell you the same thing."

"Who was she allegedly sleeping with?"

"I heard that she was seeing Caleb Trott."

"Did you ever see them together?"

"No." she answered defensively.

"What did you personally see?"

"Well, nothing. But, I've heard a lot."

"Is there anyone else who saw anything?"

She thought about this for a moment. "Well, I can't think of anyone in particular. But the hospital had a meeting a couple weeks back and told us not to gossip. So, I don't know if anyone has the guts to speak out now."

After a little more conversation, I realized there was nothing here worth reporting- just gossip. I thanked her and stood up to leave. But before I left, I asked another question.

"Sarah, just one more thing; I heard through the grapevine that you were seeing one of the doctors too. Is that true?"

She blushed instantly, the red covering her face and chest. "Who said that? Was it Carrie? She's just jealous." She was enraged and I'm glad. Maybe she'll tell me something I can use now.

"I went out with Dr. Trott a couple times but it didn't work out. He comes from money and wants to marry money. I'm not rich, you know."

She looked sad and I actually felt sorry for her. I asked her when they dated and she said last year, well before the time Joey worked there so that won't help

144

me. I thanked her and left. What a soap opera. I walked out to the parking lot and got into my vehicle. I'm looking forward to Litchfield. I hope it paid off better than this interview.

I liked Litchfield. It was a lovely little historical town with a strong 18th and 19th century architectural influence. I used to go with my mom when I was little to look for antiques when we first moved here. We'd have lunch in a different restaurant every time. I missed those days. I rolled down the window as I drove and turned on the radio to the oldies station. I liked the music from the 80's. My dad was a huge fan and I learned a lot about music from him.

The weather was warmer today, in the 50's so I'm just wearing a sweater. The sun was hitting my face just right and I drove like that for a while. As I approached Nutmeg Hill, I slowed down. The neighborhood was affluent that much was obvious. I was looking for Rose and Ted Hartley, owners of a yellow mustang since last month. She worked part-time teaching high school math and he was a retired postal worker.

Their house was a large white Dutch Colonial with black shutters and a gorgeous front yard. It was bordered by privet hedges and a black wrought iron fence. This was the kind of house I've always wanted. It looked like a nice place to live. Sometimes you can just tell that by looking.

I parked in the street and walked up the path to the front door. I rang the doorbell and waited. My cover today was that I'm writing a short story about

145

the town of Litchfield and I'd like to talk to them about living here. It was weak; I knew that, but let's see where it took me.

A pretty woman in her sixties answered the door, a chubby redhead with a quick smile. But before I could speak, two black labs pummel me and I almost fell down.

"Snickers and Oreo; get down at once; you bad boys." She said this as if she were admonishing two small human children and not dogs. They were puppies but still big and strong. I loved dogs so I didn't mind. I told her that.

"I love dogs too. Aren't they wonderful? "She was smiling again and I could already tell that I was going to like her.

I introduced myself and explained that I was driving by and wondered if the people who lived here wouldn't mind sharing some of their local experiences with me for a short story I'm writing about Litchfield for my college paper. She agreed and offered to get her husband who was in the garage tinkering with his car. I added that my dad loved cars and just bought a mustang convertible that he loves to tinker with it too. She commented on the coincidence since they have a mustang convertible too. Would I like to see it? Of course, I would and the next thing you know we are in the garage admiring their little white (not yellow) mustang.

I learned over the next half hour that they bought this mustang convertible from Mike Berger last month. Mike owned Mikes' Auto in town. He buys vintage cars and sells them for profit. They changed the color to white because they don't care much for the color yellow. I needed to speak to Mike Berger but I spent another half hour with them and took notes to make it look good and then I made up an excuse and left.

I drove around until I found Mike's Auto. It was on the edge of town. The premises looked kind of dumpy. It certainly wasn't what I was expecting. There's a few men working on cars in the large stifling garage and I asked one about Mike. He was out back in his office.

I had to walk over several grease stains and odd pieces of junk to see a corner office with wall to wall windows. Great, I could see the pornographic calendar from here. I knocked on the door and when he saw me, he looked me up and down. Mike was short, overweight and had bad hygiene. There's no other way to put it. I purposely stood in front of Miss November, blocking her from his view.

"Well, well, well, what have we got here? Are you looking for a car, little lady?"

I hated this guy already and I'd only been here less than thirty seconds. I explained that I needed information on the mustang he sold to the Hartley's last month.

"Why?" He immediately became defensive. This was not going to be easy.

"I'm interested in a car like that. Where did you get that one? It's a beauty."

"I bought it off a guy who needed the cash." He looked at me suspiciously.

"Does he have another?"

"I doubt it."

"What was his name and where was he from?"

Now, he was looking at me funny. I must have touched a nerve. So, I told him that my dad was dying and my mom and I wanted to get him a car like that before he died. I was vague about the actual disease but I hinted that it was terminal and he didn't have much time. I think he believed me because he went over to his file cabinets and searched in the drawers for a couple minutes. He pulled out a paper, read it, and handed it to me.

"I shouldn't be doing this but I lost my dad to cancer so I know how it is. This guy was from Agatha Falls."

"Do you have his name?"

"Let me see. The name on the title is Caleb Frederick Trott."

"What was the name of the person who sold you the car?"

"Caleb Trott."

148

"You paid him cash; how much money?"

"$15,000, I was being generous." He seemed almost embarrassed by the low sum he offered him. The car was worth way more than that and he knew it and I knew it.

"There were a few dings in the fender and the leather was ripped in the backseat so it wasn't as valuable as it could have been," he added to make his case.

Caleb Frederick Trott. So, he was the owner of the mustang. And he sold it after Joey died. A man in overalls entered the office just then and told Mike a customer needed to see him, so he excused himself. I quickly took my cell and snapped a picture of the title lying on his desk. I left as quickly as I could and drove home with the windows rolled down and the radio turned up.

When I got home Jake was sitting on the couch. He looked upset. "Freya, come here, look at this." On the TV screen, a picture of Mr. Hammond was being shown. The reporter from channel 5 news was speaking:

"Mr. Travis Hammond, 32 of Agatha Falls, Connecticut passed away this evening at Mercy Regional Hospital as a result of an apparent suicide attempt while in police custody. Mr. Hammond was recently arrested for a local break-in and for child pornography found on both his personal and work computers. He was fired from his job as a teacher at Evergreen High School and had several allegations of

sexual harassment against him. He was not married and had no children. Funeral arrangements have yet to be determined."

CHAPTER EIGHTEEN

The past few days were a whirlwind of activity. Since Juanita Hadley's disappearance, the town was agog with gossip. Some believed she ran off with a secret lover and others believed she was killed by the North Woods Strangler. So far, there's been no breakthrough in her case and the authorities were presuming the worst.

Former Sheriff, Linus Hadley had turned hermit. No one saw him these days. He only came out for his mail or to buy groceries. And since the murder of Quentin Ambrose, the airport expansion was put on hold temporarily. The City Council voted to investigate the assertions made by Quentin against the mayor and Juanita. There were rumors that the mayor may step down at any time.

I've had another article printed in the paper and a second visit with the FBI. This time we had a civil conversation. Maybe that's because I had my lawyer present. That always helped. The FBI was finally investigating the yellow mustang and Dr. Trott. Unfortunately, Dr. Trott left town. He supposedly went back to Colorado a few days ago to visit his dying father but never showed up. So, now he was a person of interest in Joey's killing.

I was able to get a copy of the student directory for Claremont College and not one male stunt was named Lukas. No females either; another dead end. I did find out from another hospital volunteer that last summer hydrocodone was missing several times from the ED pharmacy. They never found out who did it but they had suspicions. What those suspicions were, I don't know yet.

And one thing that was creepy. I've started getting lots of hang ups and heavy breathers calling me late at night. Last evening, Jake was at the gym, I was home alone, and the phone rang. I answered it. *Have you found the locket?* Well, no, I haven't found the locket and no one else has either. The killer must still have it. Find the locket find the killer.

The peridot ring that was left for me last week was still a mystery. Why send it to me? Who sent it? Was it the killer? I must answer these questions if I wanted to solve this mystery.

And speaking of a mystery, Jake told me that he had to go up to the attic to fix some wiring. When he got up there, guess what he found? That's right; the antique trunk Erik told me he brought to the dump. Why lie about that? Now, I'm suspicious. I knew one thing; I was getting into that attic, one way, or another.

Thanksgiving is tomorrow. I've invited Erik, Dolores, and Francesca. Jake invited Lorna. I've made three pies today and I'm exhausted. I don't know how my mom used to do this every year. God bless her. Jake was at Lorna's so I've got the house all to myself.

I'm going to take a hot bath, make some popcorn, and watch the Charlie Brown Thanksgiving special. I watched it every year. Just then, my cell rang. It said private caller.

"Hello."

"Freya Barrett?"

"Yes, who's this?"

"I'm a fan."

"A fan; what do you mean?"

"I'm a fan of your articles. Thanks to you, I'm famous now."

Oh no, it's him. What do I do? I walked over to my land line and dial 911. They put me on hold. Are you kidding me?

"Are you the person who killed Joey?"

"Maybe I am."

"What's your name?"

He laughed. "I'm not calling to help you write another article. I'm just calling to let you know that I'm watching you."

"Prove it."

"You were wearing a blue t-shirt and grey sweatpants when you went out to get the mail today."

Oh my God, he was right. I remained silent.

"Who do you love most in this world Freya, since your parents were tragically killed?"

Oh my God - Jake.

"Don't touch my brother."

He laughed again. "I can do anything I want in this town."

"Leave him out of it. This is between me and you."

"Good night Freya, sweet dreams." Click.

A 911 operator came on the line. I explained what had happened and she told me to call my local police department. Prank phone calls were not considered an emergency. Exasperated, I called the police and asked for the sheriff but he wasn't available so they connected me to the deputy. I spoke with Deputy Mott. He listened and did not interrupt.

"Freya, does your brother drive a black Chevy pick-up?"

"Why? What's wrong?" I asked.

154

"Ma'am you need to go to the hospital. Your brother had an accident and is in the Emergency Department. He's alive but has been injured."

I didn't remember driving to the hospital but when I arrived, the triage nurse gave me an odd look. I realized then that I was wearing Mickey Mouse pajamas. I gave her my name and asked for Jake. She took me to an exam room and there was my brother lying in bed with bandages around his head; and cuts and bruises all over his face.

A doctor was examining his chest. He looked terrible but he was alive. The nurse told me he was lucky; but had two broken ribs that would heal on their own in a month to six weeks. In the meantime, he needed to take it easy. I waited outside the exam room and called Lorna. I asked her to come to the hospital to wait with me. I gave her just the smallest details not wanting to upset her. I'd tell her everything once she arrived. I didn't want her driving here panicked as I did.

By time Lorna, arrived Jake was being discharged. He explained that he was driving down a hill and his brakes failed. To avoid hitting another car, he swerved and hit a tree instead. He signed the discharge papers and Lorna drove him home with me following behind.

The next morning, Deputy Mott called me and asked me to meet him at the police station. He didn't say what it was about but I had a feeling. So, I left Lorna in charge of Jake and I drove to the police department. When I got there, an officer told me they were all waiting for me. Who are they?

Sheriff Carmichael and both Agents Bent and Mooney were seated in one of the interrogation rooms. I sat across from them at the long table.

"Freya, we heard about your brother's accident. How is he?" asked Agent Bent.

She seemed sincere so I gave them all a heads up on his condition and let them know about the phone call I received last night. No one seemed surprised by what I said.

"We have something to show you and we don't want to upset you more than you are. Do you feel up to talking with us?" asked Sheriff Carmichael. I told him yes, I would speak with them.

Agent Mooney slid a manila envelope over to me. "Open it," he said. I lifted the flap and pulled out what was inside. It looked like a letter.

"Do you want me to read it?"

"Yes," said Mooney.

I opened the letter. Very neat printing, the neatest handwriting I'd ever seen. I read the words to myself.

I did not kill Joey. I loved her. I was there that night in the woods. I followed her. She went there to see Caleb Trott. By time I found her, she was already dead. I sent Joey's ring to Freya Barrett. Joey gave me that ring after I gave her my mother's locket. The killer must have taken it. I have reasons why I can't come forward just now. Find the locket. It is the answer to all of this.

I looked up. "Who sent this?" I already knew the answer, they don't know.

"We thought you might know." Agent Bent took the note and returned it to the envelope.

"I don't."

"Was this mailed to you?" I turned toward the sheriff. He shook his head. He looked embarrassed.

"It was in my mail box but it wasn't mailed."

"So, they know where you live. They must live locally then." I said.

"Well, it's no secret where I live. It's a small town, after all," he said ignoring my reasoning that the person who left the note must live in town. I was ready to go now. I'd heard enough.

"Can I go now? I've got a lot to do today. I was up late last night." As I walked to the door, Agent Bent followed me. She looked more harried than normal.

"Freya, we need your help. This person, whoever sent this letter, trusts you enough to send you something of Joey's. Can you write something for the paper to let them know they can continue to trust you? Maybe they will come forward and help us find the killer?" Up close, she looked exhausted. Feeling sorry for her, I considered her request. I was writing for the paper anyway, what one more article?

"Sure. I'll write something tonight." I saw the relief spread across her face. "Well, I've got to get home and cook a turkey." Seeing her expression, I realized she had forgotten that today was a holiday.

"Yes, I forgot. Can you recommend a restaurant around here that serves a good holiday meal?"

I rattled off the names of a few local restaurants that were open today and walked out to the parking lot. I felt my back pocket. The gun was still there. Last night when I got home, I took my dad's 9mm Glock out of the hall closet where it's been since he died. He was a big believer in home protection. I never thought about that until now.

CHAPTER NINETEEN

We're watching *SINGIN IN* THE *RAIN*. Lorna was sitting on the end of one couch with Jake's feet in her lap. Dolores left early to have dessert with friends and Francesca just left with half the chocolate cream pie. In spite of all the drama of the past week, we had a great day. Erik was beside me on the other sofa. He claimed he'd never seen this movie before and said he wasn't a fan of musicals. I believed him.

"So, is there singing and dancing through the entire movie?" he asked incredulously. I laughed out loud and explained that in musicals the characters expressed themselves through song and dance instead of only dialogue. He just nodded mutely.

The phone rang again. "Let the machine get it." I said out loud. The phone rang three times and the message played but the caller hung up before it finished. It was probably my anonymous caller. The police were able to trace a call to the closest cell tower. They used a device called a cell site simulator or a Sting Ray. It could sweep up all the phone data by imitating a cellphone tower. Law enforcement could

159

find the location of a phone without the user making calls or even texting, so much for civil liberties.

There's a tracer on my land line too and a police car parked front of our house for protection. That in addition to our security system, we should feel safe. But, I don't. For the first time in a long time, I felt very vulnerable and I hate that feeling.

The movie ended. Erik stood up, stretched himself to his full height of six feet three inches, and looked down at me. "Come to my house. I've finished the dining room, finally. I'll show you how it turned out.

"We walked out to the porch and he kissed me suddenly. I wasn't expecting it and we almost broke our noses. But the kiss was worth it.

"I'm worried about you, Freya. Jake told me what happened with his brakes. What if the killer does that to you?" There was concern in his voice. I had no answers for him – no spin to put on this. I was in danger and I brought it on myself. I lured the killer though my articles and now he wanted to hurt me. He already hurt my brother. I couldn't predict what would happen next. But I couldn't back down now.

"I'm going to be fine and so is Jake. I'm not letting this ruin our lives."

"Let me help you Freya. You don't have to do everything on your own all the time."

He took my hand as we entered his house. The dining room was off the kitchen and now painted a fresh light grey with cream trim. The dining table was at least six feet long and was positioned in the center of the room with eight upholstered chairs in cream linen surrounding it. The effect was lovely.

The lamps were stained glass and offered a soft light and a romantic feel. The wood floor was covered with throws rugs in blue and cream with hints of red. We walked through into his office and he closed the door.

"Sit down; I have to tell you something. And please don't say anything until I'm done, okay?"

I said okay and he sat down across from me at his desk. I sat back on the leather love seat and waited.

"First of all, everything that has happened between us is real. I like you and I think you like me too." He looked down when he said this, avoiding my eyes. He continued.

"I am from Massachusetts but I grew up in Canada. That is true. I'm a home renovator, that part is true too. But, I'm in Agatha Falls for another reason."

He took a deep breath. "Five years ago, my younger sister Jacqueline was dating a guy. I never liked him and I never trusted him. There was something about him; I just couldn't put my finger on it. Anyway, she was in college in Colorado at the time and I went out there for a visit. When I got to her off campus apartment, I could hear a man yelling and a

161

woman crying. The woman sounded like my sister so I broke down the door. Her boyfriend had beaten her up. She had a split lip and a black eye. Well, I lost it and beat the crap out of the guy."

"I ended up getting arrested for assault," he said shaking his head in disbelief. "My sister wouldn't press charges against him but he pressed charges against me so I ended up spending the night in jail." He walked over to a mini fridge, took out a bottle of water, and drank from it. When he finally turned to me, he had the saddest look in his eyes.

"My sister never forgave me for what I did. She wouldn't talk to me for months. One day, my dad calls me and tells me he has bad news – Jacqueline is dead. She never showed up for her classes or her part-time job and her friends got worried. The local police found her – she had been strangled. I told them right away it was him. But he had an alibi. His brother backed him up. He was rich and came from a wealthy local family, so the police dropped it. They never caught the person who did it but I know it was him. I've spent the last five years looking for him. I followed him here." He stopped and looked at me. I knew it before he says it.

"It's Caleb, isn't it?" I asked.

He shook his head. "No. It's his brother, Luke."

I gasped. Luke? Lukas. The medium was right.

"So, you've been watching him the whole time?"

"I knew wherever Caleb would be, Luke would be close behind."

"What does he look like?" I asked.

Erik went to his desk and pulled a folder from its drawer. He skimmed the papers inside and handed me a black and white photo. It showed a man with similar features to Caleb but younger and his hair was lighter in color. There was definitely a resemblance.

I started to tell Erik about the last six weeks from my own perspective. He watched me as I spoke. His eyes never left mine. When I finished, he walked over and put his arms around me.

"We are the same, we've both lost family. Whether it's a drunk driver or a crazy boyfriend, it doesn't matter. We've both suffered." He said.

"I need to show you something." Erik took my hand and led me over to the stair case and we ascended the stairs. We got to the third floor and he headed over to the attic door. He paused, removed a key from his back pocket, and opened the door. It creaked a greeting and the mustiness hit me as I entered. I sneezed and wiped my nose on my sleeve. There was an old fashioned string pull with a single light bulb overhead. The light it emitted was barely enough for us to see. When we reached the top of the stairs, Erik flicked a switch and the room was filled with light.

There had been some work done recently and the saw dust shavings on the floor showed the outline of men's boot prints. New windows had been installed and the sheet rock walls had been sanded and painted. It was a large room running the length of the top floor. There were a few boxes and a rolled up rug in one corner but in the other corner, sat the trunk. It was covered by a tarp, just like Jake said.

We walked over and Erik kneeled down in front of the trunk. I sat cross-legged beside him. He took out his key chain and using a very small key, unlocked it. He took a deep breath and lifted up the top. Once it was opened, I saw a pink and white blanket folded on top. He removed it carefully. The trunk was filled with photo albums and a few dolls and stuffed animals. I smiled when I saw a little Raggedy Anne doll.

"These belonged to Jackie. I haven't looked at them since I moved here." He pulled out a photo album and started to turn pages. I saw pictures of Erik's family. There's a young girl with long dark hair and eyes like Erik. Jacqueline looked about eighteen.

"Here's her freshman year at college. She was dead six months later." She looked happy in the photo. "You never know how much time you have. You always think you'll have so much time, but you don't."

I could tell from experience that Erik was still grieving for his sister and probably felt guilty too. Guilt was a terrible thing. It could paralyze you. After my parents died, I blamed myself. They were coming home early from the conference when they got killed. My dad had taken a short cut instead of using the freeway. I had a game that night and they were trying to get home early to see me play. I always bitched if they didn't make my games. I still felt partly responsible, even to this day.

"Erik, when I was sixteen, I lost my parents. I remember that day as if it were yesterday. I was sitting in sixth period history class. We were studying the Battle of Gettysburg. Mr. Daley, my guidance counselor came in and walked over to my teacher. He whispered something in her ear, she looked at me, and I knew it was bad. She said I needed to go with Mr. Daley. I grabbed my knapsack and walked out the door. I could tell by the way he was avoiding me that something had happened. We didn't speak and I didn't ask any questions. It was like I was trying to postpone the inevitable."

"When we finally got to Mrs. Pelluci's office, he told me. They were driving back from Stamford and were killed by a drunk driver. The police had already contacted my brother Jake and he was on the way from Boston."

Jake had studied electrical engineering in Rhode Island and had taken a job at a firm in Boston right after graduation. He came home and started his own business and never looked back. I didn't either. Neither of us spoke for a few moments. Erik continued to flip through pages, showing me his family photos. I saw his parents. He looked like his dad.

"So what's our plan?" I asked.

"Our plan is to be careful and not get ourselves killed. But from now on, we're working together. I've given all of my information about the Trott brothers to the FBI. Let's see if they believe me this time. " He leaned over and kissed me. It was a sweet kiss - nothing more. But I liked Erik's sweetness. I've never had that before. When I was with Stellen, it was all about him. I was always trying to make him happy. I never shared any of my problems with him. I tried to be the perfect girlfriend. And then he broke up with me and blamed me because I didn't need him. How ironic.

But Erik was different, more mature. I helped him put the albums back in the trunk and we walked downstairs to his living room. He walked me home and as we entered my living room, Jake and Lorna were watching the local news. There was a special report.

The Agatha Falls police are reporting the death of former Sheriff Linus Hadley this evening. Mr. Hadley failed to show up for Thanksgiving dinner earlier this afternoon and failed to return calls for the last two days. He was found dead in his home at the bottom of his basement stairs in an apparent accidental fall. His neck was broken. Mr. Hadley's ex-wife, who currently resides in Stamford, had not heard from him in the last 48 hours and became suspicious and called authorities. There appeared to be no break-in and nothing was stolen. Local police have not yet ruled out foul play. On another note, the victim's sister Juanita Hadley is still considered a missing person and has not yet been located. Anyone with any knowledge of the disappearance of Ms. Hadley should contact the Agatha Falls police department immediately.

CHAPTER TWENTY

"You don't mind me staying here, do you Freya?" asked Lorna as she walked in carrying her Yorkshire terrier ZsaZsa under her arm and wheeling behind her a suitcase large enough for me to fit inside.

"No, not with me going back to school, I won't be able to take care of Jake. Besides, its good practice for you guys when you get married," I kidded her.

She laughed and her little yappy dog barked too. I love dogs. But I like big dogs. This dog was smaller than some cats I'd known. But she was pretty and Jakes didn't mind so I don't mind either. I'm glad Lorna was here though. Jake was getting better every day but still needed help. He wouldn't allow me to hire him a nurse, so when Lorna learned that I needed help with him, she volunteered. I think my brother enjoyed having her here and I did too.

Since learning Erik's secret, I felt a sense of relief. I'm glad I'm not the only one who thought there was something going on in this town. I'm meeting with the head of the historical society tomorrow. She knew the history of St. Patrick's cemetery and might be able to help me find out who was buried in that grave.

I spoke with Margo Bent this morning and she said that Luke Trott had been in and out of trouble his whole life. He's had problems with drugs and an addiction to painkillers since a teenager. He hurt his back playing football and was accused of stealing Vicodin from a fellow student at his boarding school. He was almost expelled but his parents talked them out of it. His dad donated to the school and they dropped the investigation.

No wonder he acted the ways he did. He knew he had no accountability. His family was always bailing him out. I suggested that we check the local pawn shop to see if anyone had pawned the locket. Margo already thought of that and said that if I ever got sick of the idea of being a journalist, I should join the FBI. She thought I could have a great career in law enforcement. Now, that was something I never thought I'd ever hear. If she only knew I was still carrying my dad's gun around with me, what would she think?

The FBI was actively looking for both Trott brothers now. They were considered persons of interest. Neither had been located since Caleb took his leave of absence from Mercy Regional to visit his dad out in Colorado. The family said he visited for one day and then left. They supposedly had no idea where he is now. They also had no idea where Lukas was either. How convenient. So where could they be? Maybe the family was lying. They've covered for him in the past. Why should this time be any different?

Hair was found in the mustang that matched Joey Taylor. Thankfully, we now had forensic evidence tying Joey to the vehicle.

168

My head was aching again. I kept getting these tension headaches right in the front of my head directly over my eyes. I pinched the bridge of my nose and held it for ten seconds. I felt a little better but swallowed a couple of Tylenol just to be safe. I had a meeting this morning with Keith, so I headed over to the college

I walked into the Sentinel's office to find it practically empty "He's not back yet." It was Raj, another writer for the paper. He specialized in sports and health features but loved vintage clothes. Today, he was wearing a paisley vest and a brown derby hat. I'd never seen Raj in jeans or sweats. He didn't do casual wear. High strung but very thorough in his reporting; I respected him and his judgment.

"Is he still at lunch?" I asked. Our meeting was scheduled for 1pm so it wasn't like him to be late. I checked my watch again.

"He's at lunch with Paige," he said as he raised his eyebrows ominously.

Paige was Keith's girlfriend last year but they broke up suddenly with no explanation. Somehow, they'd managed to remain friends. Nothing like what I did to Stellen after he dropped me. I froze him out.

"Raj, I need some help from you. Can you research 1929, and see if anything happened that year in Agatha Falls? And can you see who died that year? Focus on anyone from the Ambrose or the Putnam/Ingersoll clan."

169

I did some online research on Connecticut and Agatha Falls in the 1929 and like most areas in the country; it was impacted by the stock market crash. Many of the wealthiest families lost everything. Maybe there was a link to that. Raj agreed to help and said he'd get back to me ASAP.

Keith walked in just then and I handed him my article for tomorrow's paper. This week my focus was on Joey's locket. I wanted to write about the man who loved her enough to give her his mother's locket. Maybe, it will reach him and convince him to contact me. I even included an artist's drawing of the locket in case anyone had seen it. Keith liked what I've written and said it would be in tomorrow's edition.

By time I got to the Coffee Shoppe, Francesca was already there. I'm glad because besides me, she was the best server and it was busy tonight. The next few hours fly by and by 6:30 I was on my way to the council meeting.

There was already a crowd at City Hall but I could see Ali in the back. She saved me a seat. The Beacon reported today that a new City Council President would be named tonight. According to the City Charter, in cases like this when the council present is unable to serve; a new president may be appointed by the mayor.

But, since the mayor was being investigated for corruption, the members of the council may vote one in. It sometimes was based on seniority but not always.

The longest serving member was Selene Rashid a newcomer to Agatha Falls. She moved to town a few years back from Boston with her two young sons. Selene was a single mom and had her own website design business. She was young, passionate, and not afraid to speak her mind. Selene was popular with the locals and they accepted her. That said a lot about her appeal.

The minutes were read and the meeting began. Selene banged the gavel and announced the meeting had come to order. She spoke:

"Good evening everyone. I hope you all had an enjoyable holiday and were able to spend some quality time with your loved ones. The past few weeks have been very tumultuous for our community. But, we must move forward together. We are strongest when we work together."

"My condolences go out to the families of Joey Taylor, Quentin Ambrose, and Linus Hadley. My prayers are with Juanita Hadley who still has not returned to us. Tonight, the council will vote for a new council president. I have thrown my hat into the ring and if I am elected – I will listen, I will be fair, and I will be ethical."

"Transparency is my goal. I want to bring credibility back to this office. We need to be able to trust our leaders and as leaders, we need to be above reproach. Thank you."

For the next few minutes the council votes and as expected, Selene was elected. When her name was announced for City Council President, all members of the council responded in the affirmative. The audience erupted in applause. It was no secret that Juanita Hadley was unpopular. If I've learned anything from living in a small town, don't ever underestimate the power of personal appeal. No matter how qualified you are on paper; if the voters don't like you, they won't vote for you.

The rest of the meeting pertained to the airport expansion. The council had decided to override their previous decision to allow for the expansion. They wanted an objective third party to establish a committee of local citizens to see if the expansion is truly necessary.

I laughed when I heard this because the last time the town council established an objective committee it took over a year before they came to a decision. And that was in regard to creating a local dog park. Establishing a committee was the best way to stall.

I walked out of the meeting smiling to myself. When Ali asked me what I was smiling about, I told her and she burst out laughing.

"So, what do you want to do for your birthday? It's this Saturday. You'll be twenty- no more teenager," she said poking me in the stomach.

"Oh, I don't know. I was thinking a magician, a clown and pony rides. Oh, and a bouncy house. I've always wanted a bouncy house," I said, already guessing there was a party planned.

Jake almost spilled the beans last night. But, I was looking forward to a diversion from the murder investigation. It was family tradition to have a birthday with a theme. One year, back in Chicago, when I was about six years old, my mom did my birthday to the theme of Disney characters. I especially liked Ariel from the Little Mermaid. So, my mom had a pool party and all my little friends were dressed like mermaids. And the cake looked like a giant shipwreck with characters from the movie on it. I still had a video of that party.

Since our parents died, we do it small scale. But last summer when Jake had his birthday, I made a cake and invited some of his friends over for a barbecue. I had a country music theme and he loved it. Everyone wore cowboy hats and boots. I could only imagine what he had planned for me. I couldn't wait until Saturday. I needed something light and happy to help take my mind off these murders; even if it is, was only for a little while. I desperately needed an escape.

CHAPTER TWENTY-ONE

My article was in today's paper. The title,
ANTIQUE LOCKET KEY TO JOEY'S MURDER;
was about the antique peridot locket given to her by
someone who loved her. There was even a phone
number in case anyone recognized it. Since it was
antique, it might lead us to the family who owned it,
thus leading us to the witness. It was a long shot, I
know, but I'm willing to try anything right now. The
drawing of the locket looked very detailed and
realistic. I knew a girl at school who was good at art
and she drew it, just like Emily and her mom described
it.

Professor Rothstein suggested the reason I'm
so hell bent on getting the killer of Joey was due to my
parents' death and the fact that I'd never felt like
justice was served. Well, it wasn't. The man who
killed my parents was convicted of manslaughter.

The legal definition of manslaughter was
defined as the killing of a human being without malice
aforethought. But I disagreed. The man responsible for
their death was drunk and got into his car and drove
intoxicated, killing two innocent people. He had a
history of drunk driving and had lost his license once
before. I believed that getting into a car while

intoxicated could lead to someone's death, so how was that not a form of malice? But the law disagreed.

In the great state of Connecticut, the crime of manslaughter with a motor vehicle was a Class C felony and was punishable by up to ten years in prison. But if the person had never had a previous felony violation, the likelihood of actually getting a ten year sentence was slim. The guy who killed my parents got five years, with time served. So, he'd be up for parole next summer. I wiped the tears from my eyes. I'd been thinking about my parents more than usual these days. I think it was the holiday season.

I had a meeting scheduled with our local historian this afternoon. Enid Prager-Jones; a writer with several books published about New England and the colonial era. At seventy-one, she still drove herself to work every day and was the proud owner of a 1933 Boucheron Bentley. Widowed twice, she now resided in a lovely cottage by the college and had three cocker spaniels and a Russian Blue cat named Demetri. I learned all this from Face book. She had an account with over four hundred friends.

I needed to know who was buried in that grave. Maybe the killer was leaving me a clue or else, he was just leaving a red herring. Either way, I couldn't ignore it.

Pine Hill overlooked Claremont College and most of the homes here were built in the 1920's. Their style reflected that period. Many were bungalows but Enid lived in a house resembling an English cottage.

Driving past Badger's Pond, I remembered learning how to drive on this road. There wasn't a lot of traffic up here and the view was very pretty. My dad and I used to birdwatch here. The woods were known for the native Connecticut woodpeckers that were once endangered decades ago but now thankfully, were thriving.

Enid's house was adjacent to the pond and at the end of a dead end road. It was very secluded. Her house was surrounded by the woods on two sides and the pond on the other.

There was a patio in the back of her house and a black cocker spaniel was tethered by a long leash. He saw me walking up the path and barked loudly. His tail was wagging vigorously, so, I walked over and let him smell my hand, and he gave me a little lick and sat beside me obediently. The tag on his collar read, Edison.

I rang the bell and a woman promptly answered. She was tall and slim had her hair was cut stylishly into a bob. Even in jeans and an argyle sweater, she appeared elegant.

"Freya?" I nodded and she opened the door wide letting me enter with Edison following behind. I noticed immediately, hanging in the foyer, a large black and white print from the Alfred Hitchcock film, **North by Northwest**. It was the iconic scene where Cary Grant was being chased by an airplane overhead. I smiled when I saw it. It was one of my favorite films.

"So, you've seen the movie?" she asked.

176

"Yes, it's one of my favorites and I love Cary Grant."

She smiled and shook her head in agreement. I already knew that I was going to like Enid. We entered a charmingly decorated living room. I sat down in a floral upholstered wing chair. End sat across from me on a navy blue velvet sofa. The room was full of little china dishes and souvenirs from years of travel but it wasn't crowded. The ambiance reflected the personal style of the woman who lived here. It was very warm and inviting.

"Well, you've met Edison already. Clara is over there is her basket and Calvin is in the kitchen eating his dinner. Demetri is around here somewhere. He'll let you know if he wants to meet you, he's the boss." I noticed the little honey colored cocker spaniel puppy sleeping soundly in basket by the fireplace.

"So, how can I help you?" she asked.

I gave her a brief update on my investigation into Quentin Ambrose's murder. She listened intently; only nodding occasionally. Her eyes flickered around the room as I added details and then when I mentioned the medium, her eyebrows rose in disbelief.

I mentioned the gruesome find on the 1929 headstone in St. Patrick's Cemetery. Her phone rang but she let it go to voicemail. I ended with the warning from the medium. The killer was not a psychopath. They knew exactly what they were doing. They had killed before.

She exhaled deeply. Then she got up and walked over to her desk and removed a few books on the shelf above it. She sat down and handed me one of the books. There was a family tree of the Ingersoll family and the Ambrose family. There were notations written beside the names.

"I wrote a book about five years ago and it focused on the history of colonial Connecticut. Did you know that the Ambrose family was at one time the richest family in southern Connecticut?" she asked.

"This was back in the mid to late 1700's. They were here before the Putnam's or the Ingersoll's. Quentin is the 5th generation descendant of Abraham Ambrose. Abraham was neighbors to Samuel Ingersoll, the father-in-law to Agatha Putnam Ingersoll. Anyway, they had a falling out over a land deal and it turned friends into enemies."

"Abraham owned over 100,000 acres of forest land in southern Connecticut. But Samuel owned the land surrounding it. He made it impossible for Abraham to sell off the land for a decent price because he refused to build any roads leading to it. And he intimidated anyone who wanted to buy it. As a result, the only person willing to buy the land was Samuel Ingersoll. So, he bought the entire 100,000 acres but for less than a third of what it was actually worth. This angered Ambrose, as you can imagine."

"There's not much mentioned about the Ambrose family after that until the late 1800's. By that time, much of the forest land in Connecticut had been cut down and less than third remained. This caused flooding, swamps, malaria, an excessive amount of mosquitos and eventually severe drought. The trees had been cut down to build roads and towns and the thousands of acres of trees that once stood were long gone."

She turned the page and showed me a map of southern Connecticut in the 1880's. By this time, settlers had cleared two-thirds of the states acreage for farming, agriculture and the fur trade. She explained that this is what brought on the conservation movement. She went on to explain further.

"Did you know that Connecticut was the first state to establish a State Forester?"

I shook my head.

"Yes, they were very ahead of their time. They coordinated efforts to control forest fires, which were rampant back then due to the droughts. By the early part of the 1900's, President Theodore Roosevelt warned of the eventual depletion of our natural resources. The actual conservation movement began on May 13, 1908 and President Roosevelt gave a speech stating that conservation was a national duty."

This was the first time I'd heard about any of this. "You know so much. I've never heard about any of this stuff." I offered as an excuse. She smiled.

"Yes, I know. Forestry and conservation are not sexy topics. There was a lot of politics going on with the buying and selling of land; especially back then."

"So, do you think that had something to do with Quentin's murder?

"Yes, I do. In August of 1929, there was a massive forest fire just north of here. Several members of the Ingersoll family died."

I gasped, "My God, how awful."

"Oh yes, there were rumors that the Ambrose family had something to do with it. You see, the forest used to belong to them years before."

"That was the land that got swindled away?" I asked.

"Yes, exactly; some people thought it was revenge but there was no proof that they had set it. By October of 1929, the stock market crashed and many of the families were ruined. It impacted the Ingersoll family especially. Almost everything they had was invested in the market. It just about put an end to the family. Nathaniel Ingersoll, the great grandson of Samuel shot himself to death. There were many suicides that year." She paused now and walked over to a painting hanging over her fireplace. It was a woman. She looked like someone from the past.

"Who's that?"

"This is my grandmother; Elise Hampton. She was twenty-one here. Isn't she beautiful?"

"Yes, does she have anything to do with this story?"

180

"Yes, her father was in business with the Ambrose family. She was a history buff too. I guess it runs in the family. Anyway, she kept a journal and her best friend was Eleonore Ambrose."

"She told my grandmother that Agatha Putnam Ingersoll had an affair with one of her ancestors. The family knew all about it and they adopted the baby."

"Wait, what baby? I thought Agatha never had kids."

"Not with her husband. He was too old and sickly. But according to the journal, Agatha had a son and he was raised by the father's family- the Ambrose family. Apparently, back then it was known but not discussed. In polite society, these things aren't publicized. Not like today with everyone tweeting every time they fart."

I laughed. She was right. The world could use a little more reticence right about now.

"I always thought that Agatha's philanthropy had an ulterior motive to it. Building the library and the coeducational college, I think it was done as a distraction from the gossip going around and a way to change her image. Did you know there were rumors that Agatha practiced witchcraft?"

"Witchcraft; was she a witch? I asked.

"Maybe, but it was white magic really. But in those days, if you wanted to malign a woman, you called her a witch. Elise mentioned that in her journal.

Eventually, the rumors stopped but some people believed that she cast a spell on her husband and that's why he became sick and died at sea."

Just then, a large cat wandered into the room. He walked straight toward me and sniffed my shoes. He jumped up beside me on the chair and began knitting and purling on my lap. I presumed this was Demetri.

"The Ambrose family left the state after the fire of '29 and moved out west. It wasn't until the 1960's when Quentin moved back here to attend college and stayed. The grave you speak of belongs to Levi Ingersoll; he died in the forest fire of 1929. St. Patrick's Cemetery holds the bodies of those who died in that fire."

"The northwest corner, you are describing is dedicated to those victims. You see it don't you? The killer has a grudge against the Ambrose family. Like they always say, karma's a bitch."

So, the killer puts Quentin's head on the grave of a man who died in a fire that may have been caused by the Ambrose family almost 90 years ago? And Agatha Putnam had a baby with her lover, who was an Ambrose, an enemy to her husband's family? What a soap opera.

"So, Enid, what about Agatha's family; wasn't she from Boston?"

"Yes, but her aunt and uncle lived out here with their children. Agatha was an only child and her

182

mother died in childbirth. After her father passed away, she moved here. Her uncle owned several thousand acres of farm land. She married Captain Ingersoll. He was a widower and twice her age. It was an arranged marriage; money marrying money. In fact, the name of our town was Evergreen Falls back then. The town changed it to Agatha Falls in 1792 when the college was built."

I give the girl credit, though," said Enid. "She was only twenty years old when she came here. And now, over 220 years later, we're still talking about her. As far as her money, well, when she passed away in 1838, the entire estate passed to her nephew George. He had eleven children. They married and had children and that is where the descendants come from today."

Enid looked straight at me with a very serious look on her face and gripped my arm. "Freya, I know you put a lot of faith in this medium but I don't. I believe in human nature. Human nature never changes. People hold grudges, they have grievances, and they get even. This killer, whoever it is, killed Quentin because of his family, I'm sure of it. There may be someone today, who believes they are a direct descendant of the Putnam and Ambrose affair. If they can prove that, they will be entitled to a large amount of money."

"After Eloise Putnam-Pringle died this year, she left millions of dollars to her family; Linus and Juanita Hadley, Judge Pringle and Ben Hadley. Now, Linus is dead and Juanita is missing. "

"If I were Ben and Maurice, I'd be afraid I'd be next. And as far as that teen age girl who was killed, who knows, maybe she saw something or learned something.

"People usually get murdered because of passion or they get in the way of someone. I think she got in the way. And Ambrose, well; he always had a big mouth and that's what probably got him killed in the end. He just pissed off the killer."

She walked over and returned the books to the desk and asked me if I had any more questions. She had friends coming over for dinner tonight and needed to get ready.

"Freya, if you need any more help, just let me know. If I've learned one thing about history, there are secrets in every family. If you dig deep enough, you'll find dirt in everyone's past."

She shook my hand and I walked outside. It was dark now and very cold. The temperature had dropped and snow was expected tonight. I shivered as I started my vehicle. I looked forward to getting home. Secrets; there are so many secrets. I always thought this town was bogus. All the history and the romance of Agatha Falls was a farce after all. Do I really want to write that story? And if I don't write this story, am I complicit in the lie?

CHAPTER TWENTY-TWO

Mercy Regional was decorated for the holiday season. A twenty-five foot tall Christmas tree stood in the front garden covered in white lights. The garden surrounding it was also decorated in white blinking lights.

I walked past it as I entered the hospital for my volunteer shift this evening. I was so excited. I finally got scheduled to work in the Emergency Department. The volunteer who normally worked there had the flu so I'm filling in for her. The parking lot was empty so it shouldn't be too busy tonight. I locked my bag in my locker and took the stairs down to the first floor.

Nurse Rachel Marshall was the clinical supervisor on duty. I liked her because she was easy to work with. Recently back from her honeymoon, she was more interested in furnishing her new home so she spent most of her time surfing the net and shopping. The last time I worked with her in surgical, we painted each other's nails and talked about our social lives. Tonight would be easy peasy, so I should be able to get some good gossip.

There was a lot of talk about the Caleb disappearance. Everyone had their own idea of what had happened. Some believed he'd run away, others thought he was stealing the Vicodin last summer. That made sense since his brother had an addiction. One nurse even joked that he had run off with Juanita Hadley but everyone laughed that off. From what I've heard about Caleb, he liked his girls young and Juanita at thirty-five, was ancient to him.

For most of the evening, I just stocked the linen and housekeeping closets and wiped down wheelchairs. The ED was set up with both an acute and a fast track area. I'd already been through fast track a few weeks back with my fictitious headache. That's where I met Caleb Trott. It seemed like a million years ago since that happened.

The acute area had fifteen beds and two private rooms and even one padded room for psychiatric patients. Tonight we just had a three year old with croup, a teen age boy with a broken arm and an elderly man who fell and broke his hip. He's probably going to be admitted. I worked for almost two hours straight until Rachel told me to take a break. I usually went down to the gift shop and looked around. It was your basic hospital gift shop with overpriced stuffed animals, gourmet chocolate and handmade silver jewelry made by local artisans.

"Hi Stacey, the shop looks great." Actually, the shop was crowded and over decorated, but that was Stacey's style. Stacey Nash was the gift shop manager. I met her my first night here. We hit it off immediately. She's engaged to a local firefighter and was always sharing her newest wedding plans with me.

Her theme was a white wedding. Even her bridesmaids were wearing white. The flowers were white. Everything was white. I wouldn't want that. I'd want to stand out. Isn't that the whole point of a wedding? It's your day to stand out, why share it? Oh well, it's her wedding, not mine.

We talked for a few minutes until she asked me to watch the shop so she could take a bathroom break. I agreed. There's not usually any visitors this time if night anyway. It's almost 9:00 – closing time. She ran off down the hall.

I admired the knick knacks, snow globes, and Christmas decorations. The six-foot Christmas tree was white and covered in blue lights. The obvious theme was the twelve days of Christmas and everywhere I turned; there were geese or French hens. What's a French hen anyway? She even had a partridge in a pear tree standing in the corner. Where did she get this stuff? She returned a few minutes later and started to close up.

"Hey, Freya, can you do me a favor? Could you bring these boxes down to the trash compactor? It's right by the ED."

I picked up the two boxes and walked back toward the ED. I took a left turn and went down the stairs to the ground floor and walked into the trash compactor room. I threw the boxes in and as I did, I heard something behind me. It was the door. It had slammed shut. How did that happen?

I tried to pull it open but it wouldn't budge. It must be stuck somehow. I pulled and I pulled but nothing happened. I almost panicked. Calm down, I tell myself. You can do this. I took a deep breath.

Think. My cell phone- I pulled it out and called the hospital switch board. A woman answered with a nasal sounding voice. I explained what happened and she said she'd send Gus down to get me. So, I waited. I looked around. The room was large enough to contain the trash compactor and several carts full of cardboard to be crushed. There was a slight draft blowing inside the room and I pulled my sweater snugly around me.

"Is someone in there?" I heard a man's voice.

"Yes, I'm in here. The door is stuck." I answered, embarrassed now.

The door opened with a sharp tug and there standing in front of me was the security guard, Gus, who I'd met the day I interviewed here. He looked amused. But I was not.

"What happened honey? Did the door lock on you?" He had this smirk on his face and I just wanted to get away from him. He was looking right at my boobs. He gave me the creeps. I hated situations like this. I hated having to be saved, especially by a man who was obviously a misogynist.

"Thank you." I said and I walked past him and kept walking until I got to the ED. I explained my lateness to Rachel.

"Are you kidding me? They still haven't fixed that door? I got stuck there once and so have a bunch of other people. They say they'll fix it but they never do. This place," said Rachel clearly exasperated and shaking her head.

I finished my shift and as I walked out to my car, and I saw someone running from it. I chased after them but they sprinted away. It was a man. He was wearing a hoodie so I wasn't able to see his face. I looked at my car and it looked fine but I'm uncertain. How would I know? I do know one thing; I'm not calling hospital security. I called Erik.

He answered on the second ring and I told him what happened. He told me to wait inside the hospital; he'd be here in fifteen minutes. No argument there. I walked back inside and sat in the alcove and waited for Erik to arrive. I checked my cell phone to see if I had any messages. Raj emailed me the information he found on the cemetery. I'd look at that when I get home. I couldn't concentrate right now.

A half hour later, Erik showed up. He looked so handsome in his charcoal grey coat. I went out to the parking lot with him and sat in his truck while he checked under the hood. After a while, he got back in the truck and said the brakes were fine. He looked at me and I knew there was something more.

"What is it?" I asked. He handed me an envelope.

"This was on the windshield. Does it mean anything to you?" I opened it before even thinking about fingerprints or DNA and it was a note with the same neat printing I'd seen before.

> 'Freya, you are so close.
> The best liars keep their lies
> close to the truth. Agatha
> Falls is built on a lie. Find
> the lie and you will find the
> killer. Find the locket.'

A man was sitting in his vehicle in the hospital parking lot. He was watching Freya and her male friend sitting in their truck.

She was so close now. Soon the score will be settled and everyone will know the truth. The rich and powerful always thought they could get away with anything. But this time, he was going to teach them all a lesson they won't soon forget. Everyone was accountable for their actions eventually, everyone.

CHAPTER TWENTY-THREE

Raj's information regarding the Ambrose family verified what Enid already told me. That section of the cemetery was devoted to the men who died in the forest fire of 1929, all seventeen of them. In fact, it was called the Great Fire by the locals until Grant's Department store burned down in 1962. After that, no one mentioned the Great Fire any more. Five Ingersoll's died in the fire of 1929. Arson was suspected but could never be proven. There was a drought that summer so that was eventually accepted as the cause of the blaze.

Ben Hadley asked me to stop by his house this morning for brunch. He wanted to show me his new place. So, I'm meeting him in a half hour. The Beacon had an article in the paper this morning about Mayor Garabedian. He's resigning due to the airport scandal. So, now we're having a special election for mayor. Stellen's dad was running and so was Nat Baldwin from the City Council. It should be interesting. The election was schedule for January 16^{th,} six weeks from now.

As I drove to Ben's house, I admired the local Christmas decorations. At night, this place was really something to see; lights everywhere. People go all out around here.

The downtown had miniature lights on all the trees in the city park. The bandstand in the center of the park had a lighted Christmas tree inside it and the street lamps lining Main Street were wrapped with holly and evergreen garlands. Even the fire department had a tree decorated with red and white lights in its front yard. It couldn't look more festive.

I'd like to believe it's done purely for the spirit of Christmas but it wasn't. Partly, it was for the tourists. We got a lot of them passing through this time of year from New York City and Boson because of our proximity. We'd be crazy not to take advantage of the extra revenue. Cynical, but it's true; commercialism is no stranger to Agatha Falls.

Every year, the store windows on Main Street had a new holiday theme. This year, Polly's Diner had Scrooge. The barber shop had the Grinch and the hardware store had the Nutcracker. When I was younger, I used to love to walk there at Christmas time just to see the displays. It was another local tradition here. We had a competition every year for best window display. The drug store won last year using a Victorian Christmas theme. If you weren't in the Christmas spirit when you arrived at Agatha Falls, you will be by time you leave.

Ben's house was located on Sunset Terrace; a new housing development just built in the last couple of years. Situated on a hill, it overlooked the town. His house was French provincial with a huge front lawn. There was no way he could have afforded this on his Department of Motor Vehicle job. This was definitely from his inheritance. But, it was a gorgeous house, no doubt about it. Not bad for a guy his age, I thought.

I knocked on the door and waited. The lawn was decorated with a large inflatable Rudolph the Red Nose Reindeer. Ben answered the door with a big smile. He ushered me into the dining room. It was super modern with everything gray and white with hardwood floors and very little furniture. No knick knacks anywhere. It was immaculately clean too. Not a speck of dust. I complimented him on that.

"What, you think because I'm a guy my house would be dirty? Freya, you're sexist," Ben said with a grin. We sat down and he placed a plate of blueberry pancakes in front of me.

"Is that okay? I also make really great French toast."

"No, pancakes are fine. So, what's the special occasion? You've never asked me to brunch before."

"I have a lot to tell you but let's eat first." Ben began to tell me about his family. He seemed to have a hard time at first, but then the words came pouring out.

"I was never close to Aunt Juanita. She likes to keep to herself. Besides, she never got along with my dad. She never liked my mom either. After my mom died when I was a kid, she seemed glad about it. Can you imagine? "I just nodded sympathetically. He continued.

"And then my dad had that heart attack and I lived with Uncle Linus until his divorce last year. Then I bought this place with my inheritance. So, I haven't had much of a family experience," he said sadly. I felt sorry for Ben. I wish he'd meet a nice girl who would love and appreciate him for himself and then he wouldn't have to be alone.

'Freya, I need to tell you something. I read your article about the locket, Joey's locket? Well, I think I've seen it before."

"You have, where?"

"You're going to think I'm crazy but I think it might belong to my ancestor."

Seeing the look on my face, he rushed on to elaborate. "In Uncle Maurice's house, he has several paintings of our relatives and there's a necklace in one of them that looks like the locket you described in your article."

"Is there a way for me to see this painting?"

"Hold on, I knew you'd ask that and the answer is yes. My uncle's home isn't far from here so we can drive over. But I need to warn you, he's very sick and doesn't look good these days. He has an aggressive form of brain cancer; Glioblastoma," he said this in a low voice.

I knew Ben was close to his uncle. He started fiddling with his napkin. I could tell he was upset but he continued speaking in a stronger voice.

194

"He already had a couple of surgeries last year but the cancer spread and the doctor is giving him six months. He has a nurse living with him full time. He wants to die at home. He's no longer receiving any treatment, just comfort care."

Poor Ben, he doesn't have much family left anyway and now his uncle is dying. I hugged him tightly and rubbed his back.

"I'm so sorry. But I'm your friend and I'm here for you. I know what it's like to lose family. You start to feel all alone, but you are not alone." He saw the tears in my eyes when I pulled away and wiped them away with his hand.

"Let's go see my uncle."

As he drove, I filled him in on what Enid told me about the Agatha-Ambrose affair. Ironically, he wasn't surprised.

"I've heard rumors like that for years. My granddad said the same thing when I was a kid. I think there's a journal somewhere that mentions the baby. My uncle probably still has it. I'll look in his office."

"Thanks, it would be great if I could find some proof."

"No problem. I think it's time the truth came out, don't you?" he asked me.

The truth will set you free. I thought to myself, quoting Martin Luther King.

We arrived at Judge Pringle's house. It was a Greek revival with four large white columns in the front surrounding the porch. There were two shaker style rockers on the porch painted a bright raspberry red color. They stood out against the white background and the stained glass front door. No Christmas decorations were in sight.

A dark-skinned woman answered the door and introduced herself as Nina. She led us into a room off from the foyer and it contained a hospital sized bed. The judge was covered by so many blankets; the only way I knew he was there was by his wheezing. Ben walked over and reached beneath the blankets and took his hand.

"Uncle Maurice. It's me Ben. I've brought Freya with me. Can you tell her what you told me about the locket?"

The once robust judge had now become a wizened old man with barely any fat on his body. He lifted his head and stared at me with tired blue eyes. They looked me up and down as if deciding whether to share this information with me. Finally, I passed his test and he asked Ben to sit him up in bed.

Ben adjusted the automatic bed to its upright position and Judge Pringle waved me over with a bony hand. I sat on the bed beside him smelling the aroma of old man and impending death. I wrinkled my nose and he laughed a phlegmy laugh; enjoying my discomfort. His nurse, Nina slapped him on his back. This seemed to help and he started to talk about his family.

196

"You see, things were different back then. Not like today. People didn't sleep together until marriage. If someone had an affair, it was discreet," he said pointing his finger at me. His extraneous explanation was confusing so I tried to clarify.

"Judge, what about the locket? Did Agatha have a silver locket with a peridot stone?" I asked.

"Peridot; yes, she was born in August. Agatha was born August 29th. The locket was a gift from her lover and the father of her child. She gave it to the baby when she gave the baby away. He was raised by the Ambrose family. A lot of people knew back then but never said anything about it. Besides, she was so good to the poor and she set up a school for the Irish girls who were indentured servants. Slaves really, but they called them indentured servants back then," he rambled.

"She went on to build the college and the library. She wanted to use the Ingersoll money to do good things to make up for the things they didn't. Do you understand what I'm telling you?" He asked me suddenly. He became agitated and grabbed at Ben.

"Ben, show her the painting in the sitting room, the one of Agatha." He slumped back on the bed, clearly exhausted.

We went into the sitting room and over the fire place hung a painting of a woman with dark hair and almond shaped brown eyes. She was very pretty with an arresting gaze. It was almost hypnotic. She wasn't beautiful in the traditional way but there was

197

something special about her. I got the impression she had an attitude. Maybe that's why people called her a witch. Back then, if a woman was strong and independent, they accused them of witchcraft. In fact, for someone from the 1790's she looked very modern to me. I liked her. Then I saw it, the necklace, almost coved by the lace of her dress, a silver locket with a green stone - Joey's locket. I took a few pictures. I needed to speak with Enid about this. I'd have to visit her later.

I went back into Judge Pringle's room. He seemed to be sleeping. Ben suggested we speak with Nina. So went into the kitchen and sat at the large round oak table while she poured hot water into tea cups for us. There was a plate of gingerbread cookies and some sugar cookies too, decorated in reindeer and snowman shapes covered in red and green sprinkles. She pushed the plate towards us.

"I like to bake when the Judge is sleeping. Try one; they're fresh from the oven." I bit into the gingerbread and a rush of memories came back with a vengeance. My mom and I used to bake this time of year. I haven't baked since she died. I can't take another bite so I turn to face Nina.

"So what can you tell us about the locket?"

She looked down as if remembering. Then she gave me a little smile and said, "The locket-I don't know anything about that but I do remember a young man coming here back in February saying he was a relative and the Judge throwing him out."

"Tell me all about that."

'Well, I remember it being Valentine's Day because my husband sent me roses and they were delivered here. It was so nice of him. When you've been married for fifteen years, husbands stop doing things like that. I guess they think they don't have to. Anyway, the doorbell rang and there was a young man standing there holding a manila envelope and he asked to see the Judge."

"He said he was a distant relation from out of town so I let him in. He was so polite and good looking, I didn't see the harm."

She looked at her watch. "Let me check the Judge and I'll be right back," she said and left the room.

"Ben, did you know about this too?"

He shook his head. "No, it's the first I've heard of it. But Uncle Maurice mentioned a 'scoundrel' coming around last spring so I asked Nina and she filled me in."

Nina came back in and took her seat. "He's still sleeping. Where was I? Oh yes, the boy. Anyway, he was young and cute and had manners and he reminded of my own son so I let him in. I didn't see any harm. So, I brought him upstairs to see the Judge. He wasn't as sick back then; he was still upstairs in his bedroom. So, I brought him in and then left them alone. About ten minutes later, I heard yelling. So, I ran back upstairs and the Judge was yelling and swearing and telling me to call the police. The young man was just standing there, so composed; he just walked down the stairs and out the door."

"Did you get his name?" I asked.

"No, I didn't but the Judge may know; if he can still remember. He's not as sharp as he used to be. Oh, wait a minute. He dropped this on the stairs when he walked out."

She walked over to a large hutch in the corner of the kitchen and opened a drawer. She handed me a slip of paper. It was a receipt from the Regency Hotel on Main Street. A single room for three nights back in February paid in cash. Maybe someone would remember him at the hotel. I'd have to check later.

"Could I ask the Judge a few more questions? It's very important."

We went back to Judge Pringle who seemed to be awake by now. "Where's my lunch?" He asked looking around the room. Nina told him she'd be right back with his lunch and left. I sat on the bed. I didn't want to make the judge angry or upset but I needed to know something.

"Judge Pringle. Tell me about the young man who came to see you last spring- tell me about the scoundrel" I waited. He exhaled and his shoulders slumped. He seemed defeated.

"That boy – I should have listened to him. If I did maybe, Juanita and Linus would be here now," he said sadly.

"Tell me about him. Whatever you can remember," I said gently taking his hand in my own. The Honorable Judge Pringle was now a lonely, scared, and dying man.

"Judge Pringle. Did this young man give you his name?"

Speaking very softly, the judge looked at me and said, "He told me was a descendant of Agatha Putnam and Anthony Ambrose. He showed me the journal of his grandmother and some letters from the Ambrose family. He had a DNA test that confirmed his ancestry. But those things can be manufactured." He said raising his voice.

He seemed agitated now but continued speaking... "I threw him out. He said his mother had just died and left him the papers. He said he only wanted a family. But I knew that was a lie. He wanted the money. Everyone wants money. Why would he be any different?"

He looked at me and I finally understand him. He was old and cynical, and seen it all. The young man was young and idealistic. Two different generations, two different frames of mind, no wonder they couldn't come together.

"What happened next? You threw him out. Did you tell Juanita and Linus about him?"

"Yes, I called Linus right away and my lawyer too. But, I didn't tell Juanita. I presume Linus did. Those two were very close. Too close if you ask me." I let that linger in the air for a moment. What did that mean? How close is too close?

"What about the locket? Did he show you a locket; an antique silver locket with a peridot stone at its center?"

The judge stared into space and said nothing. He seemed to be in his own world. He said something so faint we could barely hear.

'What was that Uncle Maurice?" asked Ben.

The judge continued. "He had the locket. He showed it to me. It was just like in the painting. His mother gave it to him before she died. That's when I knew for sure but I didn't want to believe it. The stories were all true and the image of our family ruined. Our works of charity; our library, the college, and the town; all ruined because that whore couldn't keep her legs together. That's what people will remember now. They always choose to remember the bad things. They always forget the good things you do."

He covered his face in his hands and stopped speaking. Nina tucked him into bed and Ben and I walked back into the sitting room to look at Agatha's painting. I reminded Ben about the journal so he went off to his uncle's office and returned a few minutes later smiling and carrying a worn leather journal.

"Here you go, if you can make out the handwriting." I took the journal and flipped through it. He was right; the handwriting was very fancy. It was dated 1931. Maybe Enid could make it out. After all, she was a historian. She must see handwriting all the time.

I won't be getting any more from the Judge today. He's clearly exhausted. I questioned a sick and dying man; and for what? To find out another piece to this never ending puzzle. But, I'm a journalist and this is what we do. We dig and dig until we hit bottom. I haven't hit bottom yet.

CHAPTER TWENTY-FOUR

I thanked both Nina and Ben for their help today. It was still light out so I drove over to the Regency Hotel. A long shot, I know, but maybe someone will remember a young man who stayed here back in February. The hotel was decorated for the holiday season. Built in the 1860's, its furnishings reflected that period.

I was last here about four years ago for a wedding. The hotel had a wedding reception here just about every weekend, especially in the summer. The restaurant had period inspired food on its menu and more modern fare like nachos, fries, and sandwiches. The hotel had a large front room decorated as a parlor. Elaborate window treatments, tea tables, and love seats adorned the room. The floor was oak planks and the walls painted light shades of blue, green, and pink.

The front desk was against the far wall and had a large curio cabinet near it filled with antique porcelain pieces. Sea shells, stones, knick knacks, and vases filled with flowers both real and artificial were in every available space. The room was crowded by today's standards but the overall effect was attractive and surprisingly cozy.

The man at the front desk was dressed in the 1860's style of dressing. He was wearing a maroon velvet waistcoat with grey pinstripe trousers and a white button down shirt. His posture was excellent. His name tag read Dwight. He smiled when he saw me approach. I explained that I was looking for someone who stayed at the hotel back in February and had a receipt. I showed it to him and asked if he could remember who stayed in that room.

"I couldn't tell you even if I knew that information. It's private. The Regency Hotel is a respectable establishment and we are very discreet here," he said with a pompous flick of his hair.

"We respect our patron's privacy and honor that. It is the golden rule of this hotel."

I handed him a rolled up twenty dollar bill and waited. He unrolled the bill and looked around. Realizing it was only the two of us, his attitude changed.

"What exactly do you need to know?" He asked quietly.

"Can you tell me the name of the person who stayed here? It's very important."

"Wait a moment, please." He went into the office behind the counter and was gone for a few minutes. I checked my cell for messages and saw that Erik had texted me. He wanted to take me to dinner tonight. Is this a ruse to get me to my surprise party?

I texted him back that I would be done by 4pm. I'd meet him at my house. By now, Dwight had returned with a post it note. He handed it to me.

"You didn't get this from me." I looked at the name written there. Oliver Keating. I've never heard that name before.

"Dwight, answer this for me. What is the registration policy for staying here? Do the guests have to show ID; even if they are paying cash?"

"Yes, we require a driver's license and a credit card to keep on file. But if a guest pre pays for their stay, they only need to show their license or picture ID. In this case, the most likely scenario is that Mr. Keating showed up without a reservation and paid for the three nights in advance in cash."

"How often does that happen?"

Dwight pursed his lips in thought. "Well, not ever really. I've been here for close to two years and everyone pays with a credit or debit card. That's just how things are done today." Yes, he's right. This guy didn't want anyone to know he was here. I got an idea.

"What about security cameras. Do you have those installed here?" I asked hopefully.

Dwight laughed. "Are you serious; cameras? This place was built in 1860. We're lucky if the plumbing and heating work."

By now, a couple had arrived to check in so I took this as my que to leave. I checked my watch. I wondered if Enid was home. I'd swing by to see.

The traffic was heavy as I left Main Street and drove toward Enid's. I looked forward to seeing her, actually. I enjoyed meeting her last time. So far, that has been one of the few perks of this investigation. As I pull into her driveway, I saw her car parked there. I didn't notice it the last time I was here. She must have had it in the garage. It was a lovely silver Bentley. I've never seen one up close before. I parked and quickly walked up to the door and knocked. I immediately heard dogs barking. The door opened a few moments later.

"Freya! How are you my dear? Come right in. I just got home from my salsa class at the Senior Center. Would you like a cup of tea?"

We walked into her kitchen with her three dogs following me and sniffing me all over. Her kitchen was small but very pretty. It looked old fashioned; maybe that's why I liked it. The wood cabinets were painted an ivory color and were long and wide and reached the ceiling. They were obviously the original cabinets. The windows faced the back yard and were covered in lace valances. A big round table stood in front of them and her cat Demetri was lying on it, staring at me. I went over to him. I realized how much I missed my cat Sasha. He smelled my fingers and continued to stare at me. I pet him and he purred loudly.

"He's playing hard to get. Ignore him and he'll be all over you. He's a male. They're all alike."

I turned around and Enid handed me a cup of peppermint tea and we went into the living room. We sat on her sofa and I began to tell her about my conversation with Ben and Judge Pringle. I showed her the picture of the necklace. I handed her the journal and asked if she can decipher the hand writing. She listened intently without drinking her tea. Eventually, she put the cup down on the coffee table and leaned forward taking in every word I'd said. When I'd finished, she just sat there for a few moments. Finally she spoke.

"I've always thought that would make a great book." I laughed.

"You write the book and I'll write the article." I said. "It's a deal," she said smiling. She started reading the journal and was able to make out some of the writing.

"Yes, it does mention the rumors about Agatha's affair. There are quite a bit here, over five hundred pages. Let me read this and I'll contact you in a couple days. Is that okay? "

"Sure, I said.

"You've already got a big chunk of the mystery solved already," she said. "This young man shows up one day to meet Judge Pringle and he has his proof of his lineage with him. The Judge throws him out and we don't hear from him since. Do you think he's the killer? Why would he kill Quentin? That's his distant relative. And Juanita and Linus; does he have something to do with that?"

208

Enid's right. What's the connection?

"Who is Oliver Keating? Does that name mean anything to you? Is Keating a founding family like the Ambrose's or the Putnam's?"

She shook her head. "I can't remember off the top of my head but I will research that for you too. But Freya, how did Joey end up with this locket? Didn't you say her boyfriend gave it to her?" Enid leaned down to pet her honey colored cocker spaniel puppy who is now chewing on her shoe.

"Her mom and sister said a man gave it to her. I assumed it was the older man she was seeing before she died. But maybe she was seeing two men. And one of them was Keating."

I'd have to check the college to see if that name matches any of the students enrolled. And I'll check with the DMV too if Ben hadn't already. He's young so it's plausible that they might have socialized. I visited for a while longer and thanked Enid and she invited me back for her Christmas party next week. I accepted. I'd love to come.

I checked my cell and there were no new messages so I drove home. I'd have enough time to shower and change for dinner and anything else my friends and family had planned.

So, I took the long way home around the pond. There was some snow on the ground. The trees were so pretty this time of year with their little dusting of snow

on their branches. It looked like powdered sugar from this distance.

I noticed a car coming up behind me so I motioned for them to pull over. This road was a single lane and only one way. The plate was Connecticut and the car was a Buick Regal. I knew because my neighbor just bought one. This wasn't my neighbor though. This car was black and theirs is silver. He's right on my tail so I sped up to drive away but he tries to pass in front of me. I swerved to avoid getting hit. Is it my imagination or was the driver wearing a balaclava mask? Well, it is winter in Connecticut, I reasoned.

The car was still behind me. He was tailgating me. So, I sped up and he did too. We drove like that for a few minutes; he'd speed up behind me and then slow down. It was almost like a game to him.

I hadn't driven this road in a while but I knew there was a turn off coming up very soon. As I increased my speed, his car drove up alongside me and suddenly passed me. He could have smashed into me if he wanted to. But he didn't. Relieved, I took a deep breath and started to relax a little. Suddenly my cell went off. It was a restricted number.

"Hello.

"Happy birthday Freya; I'm sorry I'm not there to give you my greetings in person"

"Who's this?"

"Oh, come on, you don't remember my voice?"

Oh my God, it was him. Sick of his games, I decided to play along this time. After all, the police can trace this call.

"Yes, I do remember you. Was that you just now who tried to run me off the road?"

"I was just playing with you. You've been a busy girl today. Why did you go to the judge? He's a senile old man. What does he know?"

"Wouldn't you like to know?" I said mysteriously. Long pause. No response.

"Is this Lukas? I just want you to know that I know who you are and it's just a matter of time before the FBI locates you and your brother. So, why don't you just be a man and turn yourself in? Things will go better for you both if you give up now."

There's still no response from the caller. I made the turn and pulled onto the high way leading me back to town. I relaxed.

"Well, I have to go now. So long Lukas." I hung up. There, how do you like being played with?

I drove home and parked in the garage and locked it. When I walked in, Jake was sitting up at the kitchen table.

"Hey kiddo; get changed. You have a big night."

He winked at me. Lorna was just coming out if the shower wearing her bathrobe. "I left you hot water," she said as she passed me by.

"Yeah, I'll be there in a moment." I called the hotline that Agent Bent gave me so I could trace the calls on my phone. According to the officer I spoke with, the call was traced to a cell tower on the outskirts of Agatha Falls. The number was not one I recognized but the police said they'd follow up and get back to me.

I also call Agent Bent and left her a message about the drive home from Enid's place. Hopefully the technology would work in my favor. Then, calls completed, I jumped in the shower and within minutes, I was blow-drying my hair. I heard a tap on the door and opened it. It was Erik. I pulled him in the room, shut the door, and told him everything I'd learned that day. When I finished he just looked at me.

"Well, don't you see? Joey met the descendant of Agatha and Anthony. He's here in Agatha Falls."

I'm standing in front of him with damp hair wearing a red silk kimono. For most people this would be considered a sexy and intimate moment but not us.

"Freya, you could have been killed tonight. Do you even realize that? Now, you're taunting the murderer. Where's your common sense? Are you so into the idea of becoming a famous journalist that you would endanger yourself for a story? Are you that selfish?"

I'm taken aback by his words. But he's right. I was so committed to solving this thing that I've started flirting with the killer now. What's happened to me?

Yes, it was true. I did want fame and recognition. But I also wanted to solve this crime for a lot of reasons; for Joey mostly. No sixteen year old girl should be left strangled in the woods; I don't care what she did or saw or whom she slept with. But I also wanted to be the one to solve it and I wanted the credit for doing so. Is that so bad? I have so much to say but somehow the words don't come out.

"Erik, can you leave? I need to get ready for dinner."

I shut the door and my cell rang. It was Margo Bent. She explained that the call was traced to a cell phone belonging to Caleb Trott. We spoke for a few more minutes. Finally, we were getting somewhere. The FBI had an idea of where the Trott brothers have been hiding. That's all Agent Bent would share. She ended the conversation by wishing me a happy birthday. Jake banged on my door telling me to hurry up and soon I'm back to planning what to wear to my surprise party.

Outside Freya's house, a man was walking a dog. There was nothing unusual about it; just a man walking his dog at twilight. He glanced across the street at her home as his dog sniffed the bushes and proceeded with his business. Freya visited the judge today so she knew everything she needed to in order to solve this case. She knew about the locket now and how important it was.

He was glad she spoke with Maurice before he passed away. The guy didn't look very good these days. Brain cancer was a difficult cancer to treat. His mother died from the same thing. The dog finished and he continued their walk up the street to where his truck was parked. He and the dog got in. It was dark now, so he could go to Joey's grave and visit her. No one would see him at night.

CHAPTER TWENTY-FIVE

Erik was quiet, no small talk tonight. So, I glanced out my window instead and enjoyed the snow falling softly to the ground. Christmas music was playing on the local radio station. I liked Christmas, but the season seemed to start earlier and earlier every year. When I first moved to town, Main Street used to start decorating for Christmas right after Thanksgiving. But in the last few years, the decorations went up after Halloween and Thanksgiving seemed to be missed or included with Christmas; like one holiday. Some of the stores put up all their decorations at once. By late September, it wasn't unusual to see Jack-o-lanterns, Pilgrims and Santa Clause grouped together on the same shelf.

Agent Bent said the call was traced to Caleb Trott's phone but the voice I heard was not his. She said not to worry; they had a lead on both brothers family. I sighed and Erik turned to me.

"Stop thinking about the case; it's your night to relax and enjoy yourself. You're going to give yourself a breakdown or give me one worrying about you." I believed him. He looked more tense than usual and Erik was already an intense guy

"How's the house coming?"

215

He glances at me sideways. "Are you trying to change the subject?" he asked. At last, he smiled as we seemed to have arrived at our destination.

We're at the Coffee Shoppe and there are a lot of cars parked in the lot but the restaurant itself was dark. So my party is here? I got out of the truck and walked behind Erik as he slowly walked up to the front door. Before I enter, he takes my hand in his and squeezes it.

"I'm not mad at you Freya, but you need to pull back a little from this investigation. Let the FBI do their job now. You've given them everything they need to find the killer. Try to enjoy being young."

I appreciated his concern, I really did, but I think this is what Professor Rothstein called transference. The psychological definition was the redirection of feelings from one person to another. In the medical context, it would be between a patient and their therapist. But now I worried that Erik had transferred his feelings of concern from his late sister to me. If that was true, then we would never be together in a serious relationship.

"Freya? Are you okay? What's wrong?" asked Erik standing in front of me blocking the door from my direct view. I thought I could see someone moving around inside but it was too dark and the lights were all off inside the Coffee Shoppe. I think they wanted me to walk in and they'd all jump out and scream 'surprise!'

"Do you want to go to bed with me?"

216

He gasped. He looked stunned by my question but he didn't answer.

"Well? Is that something I can expect to happen in the near future?"

'Freya, I really like you but this is not the time to talk about this?"

"Why? Is there someone else?"

He was silent. He didn't answer me and he avoided eye contact. And then I knew. I was just some girl he was spending time with until he got back to his real girlfriend.

"Is there someone else? " I asked again.

"I don't want to talk about this now. Please, they're all waiting for you inside. Don't ruin this for them."

Them, what about me? How can I face everyone in there now? But I do. I walked in and when everyone jumped out and yelled surprise, I acted appropriately surprised, smiled, and said thank you.

The lights have come on and I can see the changes made to the restaurant. It's been transformed into a movie theater. The tables have been removed and only the chairs remained. They were lined up in rows of five and there are six rows of them facing the far wall with a projector behind them.

The walls were covered with movie prints from all the movies I loved. The aroma of popcorn permeated the air and there was an actual popper set up in the corner. Rob was wearing a white apron and adding mounds of butter to the machine. Junior Mints, Snow Caps, Goobers, and Red Vines were in bowls on a long table with soda, water, juice and a vegetable platter for those foregoing the junk food.

Then I saw the cake. It was in the shape of a newspaper. And there was a copy of my article on it with my name all done with black icing to look like newspaper print. On top of the cake sat a person that I presumed was me. She had long brown hair and was holding a pencil and a little notebook.

"I love this cake! Who made this?"

"Ah hem," said Rob; my boss from the Coffee Shoppe. He was standing beside the cake with his hands on his hips.

"Rob, thank you. I love it. I didn't know you baked cakes."

He smiled, "It's a carrot cake with cream cheese frosting; it's your favorite. I'm glad you like it." He hugged me.

I started to recognize the faces of the people around me. Ali and Lincoln, Jake and Lorna, Dolores and Professor Marino were all here. They hugged me and wished me happy birthday.

Professor Rothstein, Keith, and Raj are sitting down eating snacks. The other guests are my friends from journalism class and the Sentinel. Francesca handed me a little bag and kissed my cheek.

"Freya, this is a little something I got you for protection." I pulled away the tissue to reveal a necklace. I put it around my neck.

Francesca hugged me. "It's an amulet. It protects you and keeps you safe from your enemies. I thought it might come in handy while you investigate this murder."

"Thanks Francesca. I really appreciate this."

I walked over to Jake and asked him if I could speak to him in private. We entered Rob's office in the back of the restaurant. I shut the door behind us.

"Freya, what's wrong? I could see it on your face when you walked in. What happened?"

I told him everything that happened that day; my conversation with Ben and Judge Pringle; the journal, my talk with Enid and the crazy driver who tried to run me off the road, and my conversation with Lukas. I filled him in on what Agent Bent told me about Caleb Trott's phone and then I told him about Erik. I didn't leave anything out and the next thing I knew, I was crying. He put his arms around me and held me as I told him how hurt and disappointed I was with Erik.

He listened but said nothing. I could feel his bandages around his ribs and hugged him less tightly forgetting for a moment his two broken ribs. Finally, I stopped and wiped my nose with my sleeve.

"Here, for goodness sake. Take the Kleenex will you? My God, your twenty years old and here I am still wiping your nose for you. Freya, you're still a kid and you will meet a lot of guys before you find the right one. Don't be in any hurry. Now, let's go back to the party and forget about everything else right now."

"Those people out there love you and want to show you how much you mean to them. Don't be selfish. I know it's your birthday but it's their party too, okay?"

I checked my make up in the mirror in Rob's bathroom. Then we walked out into the crowd and I put everything else out of my mind. Professor Marino was at the projector. So, I walked over and asked him what he had planned.

"Tonight I'm showing one of the best films ever made. I know you kids probably have never seen it let alone heard about it. Only an old film buff like me would know this one. So, sit down and I'll explain in a moment." Professor Marino continued to set up the film and I took a seat near Dolores and Ali. A few minutes later, the professor stood in front of the seated party goers and asked that the lights be turned down.

"Ladies and Gentlemen, welcome to the showing of one of the best films ever made. This is not only my opinion, but the opinion of many prestigious film critics. The film is called CHINATOWN and many of you will know the lead actor in the film, Jack Nicholson."

"This movie was made in 1974 before many of you were born but the subject matter is based on a true event that occurred in California in the 1930's, the California Water Wars. I won't go into that right now. The movie will explain it well enough. This type of film is known as neo-noir. That simply means new noir. Noir means a genre characterized by cynicism, fatalism, or moral ambiguity in the style of a crime story."

"What I've always liked about this film, is that it starts out letting the audience think the film is about sex or adultery, but it's not. That's a red herring. The real mystery is buried but the protagonist, Jack Gittes played by the great Nicholson deduces the real crime. I hope you like this film as much as I do and Freya, who knows, you may even get some inspiration to solve your own mystery." With that, he sat down and the film began.

Two hours later, eating cake and discussing the film with Professor Marino and Dolores who was also a movie nut; I had an epiphany. Not in the religious sense but an inspiration nevertheless. Something just clicked for me.

I realized that the case I'm working on was like the movie. At first, I thought Joey's death was all about sex or an affair with an older man but it's not. It was linked to something much bigger.

What if the man who gave her the locket was the descendant who came to town to speak with Judge Pringle? And what if, after he got rejected by the Judge, he gave the locket to Joey instead because he fell in love with her? Maybe, he wasn't the killer after all. I never thought he was anyway. So, if Lukas was the killer; what was his motivation? What was the link between him and Keating?

"What are you smiling about?" Ali was looking at me funny.

"I know that look- you're thinking about the murder, aren't you? Did the movie inspire you after all?"

"Yes. But let's not talk about that now. How's Lincoln?"

She told me that Lincoln had invited her to the Canterbury Club for next Saturday. His dad worked with Stellen's dad so he's a country club member too.

That's great. Now, I'd have someone to talk to when I go. Stellen was not the greatest conversationalist.

"Awesome Ali- do you have something to wear?"

"Yeah, I'm all set with a dress and new shoes. Why don't we go together? Ask Stellen if we can drive in one vehicle. Is that okay with you? I'll meet Lincoln there. That way we can get ready together, like we did for prom."

"Absolutely, after all we are going as friends. It's not real date. It might even take the pressure off."

I mingled with my friends for a while longer and eventually the party winded down to just a handful of people- Jake, Lorna, Rob, Ali, and Lincoln. Everyone else had left, including Erik who left before the movie.

Jake spoke with him. I don't know what he said but Erik wouldn't make eye contact with me afterward. Sometimes, having an older brother was the best thing.

CHAPTER TWENTY-SIX

When Enid said she was having a Christmas party, I thought it was going to be a small affair but as I approached her house and saw all the cars, I realized that this party was epic.

I counted as least twenty vehicles. So, I backed up and drove down the lane and parked near Badgers Pond. Good thing I wore my new winter boots or I'd never made it in this snow. There had to be at least a half a foot by the pond but the streets of Agatha Falls had all been plowed and salted.

Today was Thursday, December 7th and we've had snow every day this week. Thankfully, the front walk had been shoveled and I made it to the front door.

The music was so loud I didn't think anyone would hear me knock. I knocked really loudly, banging on the door. Finally, the door was opened by someone I didn't know but they let me in with a big smile and the smell of balsam and gingerbread hit me.

The banister was decorated with a lovely garland of evergreens and huge plaid bows. There was small tree by the front door. It was real and covered entirely in antique bulbs and ornaments.

As I entered the living room, there were people everywhere, standing, and some even sitting on the floor. Enid finally saw me and gave me a big hug.

"Freya, I'm so glad you could make it. There is someone here I want you to meet." She led me to a man I have never met before. He was wearing an ascot with a tartan vest and the ugliest Christmas sweater I'd ever seen.

"Freya, this is Donal McAllister, my literary agent. Donal, this is the young woman I told you about." He turned to me and I saw the bluest eyes I'd ever seen.

He was at least sixty years old but slim and tall and in spite of the ugly sweater, he was a doll. I extended my hand and he raised it to his lips and kissed it. No one has ever done that to me. It reminded me of something I'd seen in an old movie.

"Hello Freya. What a lovely name for lovely lass. I hope you don't think me too forward but you have the loveliest hazel eyes I've ever seen." His brogue was thick but I loved it. He sounded like Sean Connery. I told him that and he leaned forward and kissed me on the cheek.

"Now, now, Donal; leave the girl alone. She's young enough to be your granddaughter," said Enid protectively putting her arm around my shoulder.

"This young lady has a question for you about the Keating family. Freya, I gave Donal the journal to

225

read. And he picked up some important information in it."

"What did you learn?" I'd been anxiously waiting for the results all week. When Enid called me Tuesday to tell me she had handed the journal over to a friend to look at, I was almost afraid it would get lost or stolen.

"Well, lass, the name Keating may not be one of the founding families of this area, but they are back in Ireland. I'm Scotch-Irish myself so I took an immediate interest in the name, of course. In the early 1920's, Mary Ann Ambrose married John Keating and they settled in nearby Rhode Island and went on to have seven children. I'm sure that this Oliver Keating is related to them."

"Freya, I have compiled a list of the descendants from that family. Here are their names. Does anything ring a bell?" Enid handed me a typed list of at least two dozen names. I skimmed them, not recognizing any, except one. There it is. I know this person.

"Enid, where is the journal? I need it. I'm sorry, I don't mean to be rude, but I have to leave now." I said quickly.

She hurried off to her office while Donal regaled me with stories about his four ex-wives and his current fiancé who is half his age. I wasn't even listening to him. I was too excited. I know who the descendant was.

Enid handed me the journal. "Freya, what is it? You look like you just won the lottery."

"I have," I said as I hurry out the front door.

It's almost impossible to run in the snow to my vehicle but I tried my best. I hopped in and started to warm it up. I texted Ben telling him I needed to see him right away. He should be the first to hear my news. I drove to his house as quickly as I could without managing to get a ticket. I parked behind his vehicle and jumped out of the Escort so quickly that I slipped on the ice in the driveway. I steadied myself and ran to the front door and banged on it several times.

"Freya! My God, what's wrong? I just got your text." He said as he let me in. He looked at me oddly and I glanced at myself if the foyer mirror. My hair was all askew, my mascara was smeared, and my coat was buttoned the wrong way. But I didn't care.

"Ben, sit down, I need to show you something."

I explained as quickly as I could what I'd just learned from Enid and Donal. I handed him the list and he scanned it.

"Freya, I don't know anyone with these surnames."

"But I do." And I tell him what I know.

Ben looked at me uncertainly. "Are you sure it's him?"

"Yes. It has to be. It all makes sense now. So, here's my plan." I spent the next few minutes telling him my idea and slowly he started to smile and shake his head. He agreed it was a great idea. Then, I called Margo Bent and asked her to come to Ben's house. We needed to talk.

While we waited for Margo to show up, Ben told me that he was running for City Council. Nat Baldwin had stepped down to run for Mayor and he had a good shot of getting it too. He was much better liked than Mr. Sorensen. Ben was also considering donating money from his inheritance to some local charities and environmental agencies.

"That's wonderful Ben; good for you. I wish I had that kind of money. I'd love to help people who really needed it."

With my scholarship and part-time job at the diner and my occasional babysitting jobs, money was tight. When my parents died, there was some money left to Jake and me but mine was in a trust until I'm twenty-five.

We are both co-owners of the house but Jake takes care of those bills. My money goes for school and my car. Jake does very well with his business but that's his money. And besides, I didn't want someone else paying my bills for me. I'm an adult woman; I can take care of myself. But, I couldn't wait until I graduated and started making real money.

As soon as Agent Bent arrived with her partner, agent Mooney, I told them everything I knew and shared Judge Pringle's journal. I was afraid that if we approached this young man too enthusiastically, he'd bolt. So, I suggested that Ben and I approach him first. The FBI wanted him because he was a possible witness to a murder but we needed to question him too. I wanted to know about his ancestry, since the secret love affair between Agatha and her lover seemed to be the reason this whole thing started.

Margo agreed but wanted Sheriff Carmichael there for back-up. She called him and quickly relayed my plan. But first, we needed to find this guy. I know who he was but not where he lived. But the FBI took care of that by tracing him to a local apartment not far from Claremont College. I'd agreed to drive there with Ben and the FBI and police would follow in unmarked vehicles. I texted Jake to tell him not to wait dinner for me and then we were off.

We were approaching the street where he lived so we parked on a side street. The FBI and the Sheriff parked down the road from us. I took a series of deep breaths as Ben and I walked the short distance to his apartment. When we got to the front door, we just stood there. Finally, I knocked on the door. We could hear someone inside. And then, the door opened.

I looked at the young man who was at the center of all of this. He was dressed in jeans and a sweat shirt. He looked like any college student.

"Hi Freya, I wondered what was taking you so long." He said good-naturedly, acting as if he was almost expecting us.

229

"Would you like to come in? What can I do for you?" he asked politely.

"Don't you mean what we can do for you, Jon?"

He didn't say anything for a few moments so I waited. I looked around the apartment and I could see his security uniform for the hospital hanging from a hook. His ironing board was out. I saw no personal items or photos anywhere.

"I suppose I should introduce myself, I'm Ben Hadley." He extended his hand and Jon shook it.

"So, what do we call you; Jon or Oliver?" I asked.

"Jon is my middle name. I go by that. I never liked the name Oliver. My mom named me after a character in a movie. I think it's called Love Story?"

I knew that film, my mom's favorite.

"Yes, Oliver Barrett; he was a college student at Harvard who came from money and fell in love with a poor girl on scholarship at Radcliffe. She dies at the end."

I looked him in the eyes. "The FBI needs to speak with you but Ben and I wanted to talk to you first."

"What do you want to know?" he asked casually.

230

"Everything, are you kidding?" I couldn't wait any longer. Just then a little dog walked out from behind the sofa; a mutt, but cute as hell.

"Come here Biscuit." Jon rubbed the little dog's ears. "This is Biscuit, he's my roommate." Jon sighed and sat down on the couch. We sat beside him. He began to talk.

"Well, I suppose I should start at the beginning. My mom died last year from brain cancer. The same form Maurice has, ironically. She always intended to come with me to Agatha Falls so I could meet my family, but she died. She was a history teacher at a college in Arizona where I grew up. She researched my dad's family after he died and found the connection between them and the Putnam's."

"Our plan was to come out here when I graduated high school. But she got sick and that was put on hold. After she died, I came here and brought the journal, letters, and the locket as proof. I even had one of those ancestry tests with the DNA and thought that was enough. I really let myself believe that I would be wanted. But I was wrong." He paused for a moment but Ben and I remained silent. He soon continued.

"Judge Pringle threatened to have me arrested. I'm eighteen, I don't have any money or family, and I'm in a town where I don't know anybody. I didn't come here to fight. He was talking about lawyers and taking me to court. So, I left and went back to the hotel. I was getting ready to leave for Arizona when I stopped in Polly's Diner to get something to eat before

I boarded my bus. That's when I saw her." His face lit up when he mentioned her. I leaned forward in my seat.

"She was dropping off fliers for a school play she was in; Oklahoma. Anyway, she started talking to me and the next thing I know is I'm on my way with her and her friends to the hospital."

"She was signing up to be a volunteer. That's when I saw the job opening for the security guard's position. I had done some work like that back home for a department store. I want to be a police officer, you see. So, it made sense. I got the job and stayed in town. I forgot about the whole Putnam family connection and started dating Joey. I got an apartment off campus and enrolled at the college. Everything was great. Then, one day, in June, she breaks it off with me. She tells me she just wants to be friends. I gave her the locket then. I thought that might make her change her mind."

"But I found out she was dating a doctor, rich and old enough to be her dad. Dr. Trott was a player and I told her that but she didn't want to hear it and stopped talking to me for a while. Then, one day she came to me and told me she was scared. She had seen something terrible."

I stopped him then. "When was this?"

"She told me in July. But the thing happened before that. I don't know the date. I think it was the beginning of summer. Why? Does that matter?"

"It might. Please continue."

232

"So, she gave me her ring then, it was a silver, peridot ring. Joey was born in August, you know."

He paused then and went into his kitchen. He grabbed some Cokes and handed one each to Ben and me. He opened the bottle and took a long drink.

"She wouldn't tell me what happened but I heard a lot of stuff about Trott. Drugs were missing and it was believed that he was taking them. A camera was installed and he was caught in the Meds Room a few times. Administration approached him but he was smooth and denied it. By time he went to see his dad in Colorado, the hospital had suspended him."

"Why didn't they say something to the police?" asked Ben, clearly agitated.

Jon laughed. "Image, dude, it's all about image with them. There's a lot of stuff that happens there. You'd be surprised."

"So, then what happened?" I asked.

"Well, one day, Joey came to me and asked me to follow her. She was meeting Trott and wanted to get him to admit something and she was going to record him on her phone. I told her it was too dangerous but she never listened to me. She wouldn't listen to anyone. She always thought she knew what was best. Anyway, she used to go out to the Old North Woods to be alone with Trott and she asked me to follow her out there and I agreed."

" He'd drive out there and park on the road and go the rest of the way on foot .She'd walk from town so no one ever saw them together. That night, I followed behind and made sure he didn't see me."

"What type of truck was it? What was the color?"

"Grey, I think. But it was an older model. Trott has several vehicles. He used his mustang in the summer but that night, he drove the truck. He also drives a Trans Am."

"So, what happened next?"

"Well, I followed her out there and she waited for him. It was a warm night and kind of sultry. Not your typical October weather."

"What day was this?"

"Friday, October the 13th. Ironic, isn't it? Anyway, she walked a little ways to a clearing near some trees and I hid in the bushes off to the side. After a little while, I saw Joey run over to a man and hug him. It was dark but there was a full moon. Otherwise, I couldn't see.'

"Then suddenly she turned to run away but he grabbed her from behind. She seemed scared all of a sudden."

"Who grabbed her?"

"Trott or at least I thought it was him at the time. I couldn't see exactly what was happening but then when I realized she was being choked, I tried to yell and just as I did, she slumped to the ground."

He stopped then. Ben and I remained silent. He continued.

"I was frozen, I couldn't move. I saw the guy who choked her take something from her neck. It was probably her locket. She never took it off."

"He leaned down and checked her pulse. And then he walked to his truck. He just left her there on the ground," he said incredulously.

"I walked over and felt for a pulse but I couldn't find one. She was dead."

"Why didn't you call the police?" I asked.

"The police; you mean the sheriff? Linus Hadley; the guy Pringle called to have me arrested back in February? No way. I couldn't trust him. He'd probably say I did it. And who'd believe me? I'm from out of town, I didn't grow up here; I know how this place works. If you're an outsider; you're screwed," he said bitterly.

"I went back to my apartment. I knew I was too late to save Joey so I started following Trott. Being a hospital security guard made that easy. He had a brother, Lukas with a drug problem. Now, I'm sure that's the guy who killed Joey. It was too dark for me to see but it had to be him. Whatever she saw at the hospital, she told Trott and he got his brother to shut her up."

"We need to call the FBI in now. You have to speak with them." I said. I texted Agent Bent to let her know Jon was ready to speak with her.

"So, why send me notes? Why not just talk to me; why all the secrecy?"

"I didn't know if I could trust you. But after reading your articles, I knew you were a good person who cared about Joey. You wanted justice and so do I. I'm sorry if I made it hard for you but after being threatened by the judge and the sheriff, I was scared. I'm sorry Freya."

There was a knock at the door and Agents Bent and Mooney entered with Sheriff Carmichael. Ben and I left and asked Jon to call us later. I was exhausted. All I wanted was to go home, take a hot bath, and go to bed.

The day had been long but productive. A lot of questions had been answered but I didn't feel any better. I thought by this point I'd feel, I don't know, do I dare say, fulfilled? If anything, I still felt that empty feeling I had gotten used to living with. Maybe when Joey's killer was apprehended, then I'd feel complete.

CHAPTER TWENTY-SEVEN

When I arrived at my house, Stellen was there. He was the last person I wanted to see right now. I was still hoping for a hot bath, some cold pizza, and bed.

"Hey, what's up? " I asked.

"Freya, Stellen needs to talk to you about something. Why don't you go out on the sun porch?" said Jake, readjusting the pillows beneath him.

I went onto the porch with Stellen and shut the door behind me. He looked nervous, as usual. I never noticed when we were dating, but he had a shifty look about him. Of course, at that time, I thought I was in love with him. He lied to me too. Just like Erik. What is it with men?

"Freya, my dad's running for mayor. Have you heard?"

"Yeah, that's great," I said, not really meaning it.

"Thanks, but the reason I'm here is – well- I need your help. Could you write something nice about him for the college paper?"

He avoided eye contact with me. I'd never known Stellen to be even vaguely political. I guessed that all changed when your dad was running for office.

"What kind of article? Do you want me to interview him?"

"Well, yeah, if you could. He thought, I mean, I thought, if the college students voted for him, it might garner him more votes. You know, Nat is a coach at the college and a part-time athletic trainer at the hospital and he's been on the City Council for a long time. People already know him. But my dad isn't as well known."

I was tempted to say no, right off the bat, but I didn't. Instead, I made a recommendation. I decided to pass the buck.

"You need to speak with Keith about this. He's the editor at the Sentinel. He is the one who makes the decisions about what gets printed. I'll give you his number. Actually, it would be a good idea for both the candidates to be interviewed." I could see from his expression that he didn't like the idea of both candidates being interviewed.

"Thanks. I appreciate that. So, what time do you want me to pick you up Saturday? The party starts at 7pm."

"How about 6:30? Oh, and Ali is riding with us. I didn't think you'd mind. You can pick us up here."

I could tell he didn't like that either. I walked him to the front door and said good bye. Jake was watching the local news. There was an update on the disappearance of Juanita Hadley. Apparently, the police were now calling it a homicide. They had reason to believe that she had been murdered by Lukas Trott, but they didn't give any details. My God, I wasn't expecting that. I thought for sure she'd turn up alive sooner or later.

The next news segment mentioned the Regency Hotel. CPI was coming to Agatha Falls to film a paranormal investigation into the hauntings at the hotel. CPI stood for the Connecticut Paranormal Investigators. They were a team of ghost hunters who specialized in ghost investigations. They filmed them and made them into mini movies and showed them on our local station and on their website. Their last investigation was about St. Patrick's Cemetery.

There were five guys who do it as a hobby. But they took it very seriously. Hmmm, I wonder if I could interview them for the paper. I'd have to ask Keith about that. .

I called Dolores right after my bath and told her all about my conversation with Jon/Oliver Keating.

"Freya, you did it! You solved the mystery. You should be very proud of yourself. You're a regular Sherlock Holmes."

"Well, partly solved. Yeah, I'm looking forward to the end of this. I still want justice for Joey. I'll keep you posted."

Just as I was dropping off to sleep, I felt someone shaking me. It was Lorna.

"Lorna, what is it?"

"Oh my God, I've been calling you guys. Doesn't anyone pick up his or her cell? Caleb Trott was arrested tonight. He was in Bridgeport at a Bed and Breakfast. Not the place I'd pick to hide if I were on the lam."

"What about his brother? What about Lukas?" I asked.

"No Lukas, just him. I learned about it from Milly. She takes spin class with me. Anyway, she heard about it before she left the police station tonight. He's being questioned right now. It just happened less than an hour ago."

According to Lorna, Caleb had gone out to buy gas and was stopped by the police for a broken taillight. They ran his license as was protocol and his name popped up. Thank God for broken taillights.

I want nothing more than to call Emily and her mom to tell them that we caught Joey's killer but it was still too soon. I fall asleep feeling a lot less empty.

CHAPTER TWENTY-EIGHT

It snowed heavily last night leaving at least six inches in its wake. I woke up early to shovel the front walk for the mail carrier and the paper boy. Since Jake's injury, that left the shoveling up to me but I didn't mind it. It gave me a chance to get some exercise and think. Tonight was the party at the country club. Ali's coming over early to get ready. It felt like the junior prom all over again.

I swept the snow to the side of the walk and worked quickly since the snow was fresh and soft. It was the kind of snow we used to go sledding in when I was a kid. Jake would pull me on my little red sled though the forest behind our house until we arrived at the big hill alongside the falls.

We'd climb up and slide down over and over again until our fingers and toes became numb. One year it was so cold, the falls froze over. There was a picture of it on the front page of the newspaper. I cut it out and saved it. I think I still have it somewhere in my desk.

Jake was feeling a lot better these days so Lorna was going to return to her house this weekend. I knew she loved Jake but she missed her house and her house plants and her own space. I totally understand how she felt. It must be hard for people who are married. I don't think I could live with anyone. I like being on my own too much. I think I could be married if we lived separately. And I definitely could not share a bathroom with anyone.

"What are you thinking about? You look stressed" said Jake adding a gigantic pat of butter to his stack of waffles. I envy men and their metabolisms. I had one waffle on my plate and he had at least four.

"Oh nothing, I'm great. The party at the country club is tonight. Ali's coming over around 4:30 to start getting ready. Are you and Lorna planning anything fun tonight?"

"I'm going stir crazy just lying around in the house all day so we're going out to eat and to see a concert. What time are you planning on coming home?"

"Late. Probably close to midnight. I'll text you."

I heard the paper hitting the porch so I hurried off to grab it before it got all wet from the snow. There's a black SUV parked in front of our house again. It looked like the FBI's vehicle. So, I stood by the front door and waited and sure enough, there are Agents Bent and Mooney walking as carefully as they could over the snow pile the plow left in front of my house. I opened the door to them as they walked in bringing the cold morning air with them.

"Good morning Freya. Can we speak to you and your brother? We'll do this as quickly as possible." Agent Mooney was all business so I ushered them both into the kitchen and offered them a seat and poured them each a cup of coffee. Agent Bent took a sip and sat back in her chair. She looked exhausted.

"Would either of you like some waffles? How about some toast?" I offered.

"Oh, no thank you, we've had breakfast. We wanted to fill you both in on something that happened last night. But knowing you Freya, you probably already heard about it."

Agent Bent appraised me in my Yankees t-shirt and sweats and I gave her a once over in her grey, business suit. If being an FBI agent meant that I'd have to dress like that, forget it.

"Well, actually, I might have heard something relating to a Dr. Caleb Trott being picked up for a broken taillight in Bridgeport, of all places."

Both agents looked at each other over their coffee cups and each took a sip simultaneously.

"Okay, so what's up with Jon? Have you spoken to him yet? After Ben and I left Thursday, we didn't hear anything and there's been nothing in the news either."

She nodded. "I'm not able to say anything specifically about that. But yes, we did take his statement."

"The reason I'm here though, regards your safety. We have reason to believe that the killer, who we now believe is Lukas Trott, will strike again. And we have reason to believe that this time; it will be you that is his target."

"Now, wait a minute; if you know my sister is in danger than do something about it," said Jake.

"Mr. Barrett, we are thinking of your sister's welfare. And I can't force her or you to do what I suggest. So, please be careful, especially for the next 48 hours. I've asked the police to follow you the next time you leave your home. Do you have any plans for the weekend?"

I explained about the party at the Canterbury Club." She stood up and Agent Mooney followed as they walked to the front door. "That's no problem. We can arrange some surveillance. Just act like you normally would." Yeah, right, I think.

Jake leaned over and whispered something in Agent Bent's ear. They spoke for a few moments before they left.

He shuts the door and turned to me. "Bring the gun with you tonight."

I gasped. He knows I have the gun. How does he know that?

"What gun? " I tried to ask nonchalantly.

"Dad's gun; it's been missing for a few weeks now. I found it in your bag. Just make sure you don't shoot unless you have to and for God's sake, make sure the safety's off." He notices the expression on my face.

"Yeah, I know you have the gun. Just make sure you've got a permit to carry it or you'll be the one in jail."

"I have a permit and I've practiced at the shooting range."

"Good." He walked into his office and closed the door behind him. My brother was amazing. He knew everything. Maybe he should write for the paper and I should build houses.

CHAPTER TWENTY-NINE

I mentally prepared myself for this evening by concentrating on the real reason I agreed to go with Stellen in the first place. I was going purely for information. But in light of recent developments in the Joey Taylor murder, that wasn't necessary now.

I'm sure the people invited will be the elites of Connecticut business and politics. From experience, I knew that they were not the easiest people to mingle with. As soon as they found out I didn't have a name or a trust fund, they'd ignore me. The last time I attended one of Stellen's dad's parties, I sat by myself most of the evening. His family wasn't rude exactly, they just froze me out. Sometimes, being ignored was the worst thing one person could do to another.

Stellen's dad, Lars, was in real estate and investments. His Uncle Nils was a State Senator. And his mom, Ingrid was a former model who now made her living as a social events coordinator. His older brother Johan was the owner of the Regency Hotel.

The family originated from Sweden and moved here when Stellen and Nils were college students. They liked Connecticut and stayed. Lars met Ingrid back home in Gothenburg while he was visiting family.

They were good people, just very smug and entitled. Knowing this about the family helped me to empathize with Stellen. His family had high expectations for him and sometimes the pressure was too much. He needed to stand up to them but he wouldn't. I don't know if it's the culture or the family itself. When Lars said something, they all jumped. Now, he was running for Mayor and God help Stellen. I was certain that his dad forced him into helping the campaign. If Lars lost, there would be hell to pay.

Lincoln dropped Ali off an hour ago.

"What do you think?" she stood before me modeling her dress. It was a little black dress with spaghetti straps. She looked great but when you're a size two, you look good in everything.

"You look beautiful." I said.

"And so do you. Freya. You should wear that color more often. I love that shade of blue on you."

I was wearing a navy wrap style maxi dress. My feet were killing me but I looked as tall and sleek as I possibly could.

"Thanks. It's been over a year since I wore formal wear. Let's see if I can walk in these shoes." I practiced walking up and down the hallway outside my bedroom. I tripped a few times but soon gained my footing.

"It's a little after six, what time is he coming again?" This was only the fifth time she's asked me since she got here.

"Six-thirty, don't worry. Stellen is never late." That was one good thing about him. Just to be on the safe side, I texted him that we're ready and he texted back almost instantly. He was just leaving.

It just started to snow. I gave Ali a heads up on the weather and we grabbed our coats and sat in the living room. I flicked on the outside lights and watch the snow squall. Great, the one time I'm not wearing boots. I texted Jake to remind him I'd be late tonight. Since he was out with Lorna, we might not see each other until morning.

Twenty minutes passed before headlights approached the house. The squall had thankfully stopped by now. But, it left a slight dusting of snow on the ground. I let Stellen in and he appraised me with me with the same blue eyes I used to find so irresistible. Now, I only noticed them for their vibrant color. Gorgeous eyes, no doubt about it but I didn't feel the way I did before he hurt me. The old feeling of excitement was now replaced by a sort of numbness. Ironically, pain was the best analgesic.

"You look so beautiful. I love you in that color." He stood before me in a dark grey suit. He looked tall, strong, and handsome.

"See, I told you." Ali chimed in, reminding him of her presence.

"Blue is her color. Stellen, how do I look?" She twirled around showing off her petite figure and Stellen appraised her as he would a little sister. He nodded and gave her an appropriate compliment and Ali beamed. She loved attention and she knew how to get it. Being an only child does that to a person.

I locked the door behind me and we walked to the car. He brought his dad's Mercedes tonight. Ever the gentleman, he opened the door for both of us and we drove off in a flurry of excitement matching the sensation of prom night.

The drive to the country club took us past Potters Mill, circa 1846; a place no longer in use and only frequented by history buffs and ghost hunters. The mill was closed down in the early 1940's.

The owner, Barnaby Potter, lost almost everything in the Stock Market Crash. The mill closed eventually; like so many other New England mills due to changes in technology and an educated work force looking for careers and not just sweat shop jobs. Barnaby never invested any of his profits into the mill and it soon became old and run down and couldn't compete with the newer machines being built every day. Over the years, a few out of towners bought the place attempting to fix it up but nothing ever came to fruition. An antique mall, a restaurant, and a Bed and Breakfast; all attempted and all failed. The place was unofficially cursed.

We pulled into the parking lot of the Canterbury Club and the place was ablaze with light. They could probably see it from the next town. The restaurant was on the second floor and the entire structure ran about 75,000 square feet; almost two acres.

It was definitely the largest building in Agatha Falls and it sat on seventy-five acres of golf course that abutted Pine Haven, our neighboring town. I'd been looking forward to seeing this place since it opened. While the country club was only opened to members, the restaurant was open to everyone.

We walked up the staircase and into the vestibule. An attendant took our coats and wraps. She handed us each a ticket and Stellen led us over to the bar area to look for his family. I glanced around but I didn't recognize anyone yet. I didn't even see Lincoln. Ali, almost reading my mind became agitated that he might be late, as was usual for him.

"Where is he? He better not be late." Oh, oh. I hope she didn't get pissed because once she's in a bad mood she stayed that way.

Stellen found his parents in the crowd and we went to greet them. Lars and Ingrid made an attractive couple. Early fifties, lean, trim and impeccably dressed. I recognized Lars familiar comb over. I wish he'd just shave his head. I don't understand bald men. They persist in combing one piece of long, limp hair and wrapping it around their head.

Ingrid on the other hand has used so much hair spray that I could smell it. My nose tingled from the chemical harshness of it. Her ash blond shoulder length hair was in a chignon and there was enough product holding it together, it didn't even look real. My hair was French braided and held back from my face with an antique onyx clip. Little wisps of hair hung gently in my face. I wasn't a fan of severe hair styles.

Stellen introduced me to his parents and they acted like it was the first time they've ever met me. I played along just to be polite. Thankfully, Lincoln had arrived with his parents and Ali was back to normal. We all sat down at a huge table and awaited Johan and his wife Greta.

The dining room was beautiful. The ceiling was barrel-vaulted with crystal Art Deco chandeliers hanging overhead. The floor was checkered grey and white terrazzo tiles. The overall style was Georgian with a large white marbled fireplace at one end of the room with a gold leaf octagonal mirror above it.

The balcony windows were long, floor to ceiling with multi panes and they surrounded the room giving a view of the country club below. The room was light and airy with colors of white and gold accents. No, wonder so many people had their wedding receptions here.

"So, Freda, what do you do?"

It was Lars. He's already had two glasses of champagne. Stellen looked at me with pleading eyes. This was going to be a long night.

"It's Freya and I'm a student at Claremont College. We've met before Mr. Sorensen. In fact, Stellen and I used to go out."

"Oh, oh, well, how's school going then? What's your major?"

"I'm studying journalism with a minor in psychology. I write for the college paper, the Sentinel. Maybe you've seen my articles in the paper about the North Woods Strangler."

"Oh, is that you? My God, you're a regular Agatha Christie. My goodness you put the cops to shame in this town. But I better not say that now out loud since I'm running for mayor. Did my son tell you? I'm running for mayor. And by God, the people of this town would be lucky to have me. Do you know that I am self-made? That's right. I came here with only the clothes on my back and look at me now."

I did look at him. His eyes were bloodshot and his face was red and puffy; a sign of alcoholism if ever I saw it. And as far as him coming here with only the clothes on his back, that was bull. His father was a rich Swedish industrialist who gave him money to start his real estate business. He was thrown out of Yale for college hazing; a student almost died. So, he came out here and stayed, like a lot of people do. If it weren't for daddy, he'd have nothing. But I didn't say that. I just nodded and humored him. Sometimes that's the only thing you can do.

By now, Johan and Greta had arrived with Nils and his fiancé, Desdemona. She seemed nice and smiled at everyone. By the look of her, she must be a model; tall, super skinny with blond hair and blue eyes. I recognized a pattern here. How did Stellen ever choose me? I'm the antithesis of a Nordic Goddess.

252

I guess opposites do attract, even if it is temporarily. More introductions were made and the meal was served. Pheasant with risotto, roasted asparagus, and cauliflower with apricot sauce and a beet salad with goat cheese were placed before me. I've never had pheasant and I can't remember the last time I ate a beat but I took a bite and everything was delicious.

Nils stood up and tapped his glass with a little spoon getting everyone's attention. It looked like he was going to make speech about his impending wedding.

"Ladies and gentlemen, before we eat this wonderful meal, I'd like to say a few words about my brother. A self-made man and entrepreneur who came here over twenty years ago, a stranger in a strange land, he conquered it with pure drive and vision."

"His real estate business is the most successful in all of New England. His business acumen is renowned. He is liked and respected by everyone. Now, he has decided that he is needed by this town."

"He is running for mayor of Agatha Falls and I ask each and every one of you to give him your vote and your support. Together, we need to make Agatha Falls great again."

Where have I heard that before? Another millionaire who wanted to help the working class, God save us. But the audience seemed to agree and they clapped and cheer. I guess as usual, I'm in the minority.

253

Nils sat down and we all resumed eating. Soon, dessert was served. Lemon and lime mascarpone tarts with raspberry sorbet. I could hear a piano and the soft strains of Clare de lune filling the room.

I glanced around the table. Ali was sitting beside Lincoln, Desdemona was to my right, and Stellen's sister in law was to my left. His parents were across from me with Stellen beside them. His mother was barely picking at her food. She didn't look happy. She looked bored. She noticed me watching her and she immediately smiled a fake overly happy grin. Well, I guess what they say is true. Money doesn't buy happiness.

Soft jazz began to play on the piano. People took to the dance floor and Ali and Lincoln got up from the table to join them.

"Will you save me a dance?"

It was Stellen. He'd been quiet all night until now. I'd almost forgotten he was here.

"Dancing? You didn't say there would be dancing." Suddenly I was hit with a wave of anxiety. I couldn't dance. Even when I went to my prom, my date and I just stood around or we sat at our table. I didn't dance.

"It's just a slow dance. I'll lead. Don't stress." And the next thing I knew, I was being led to the dance floor by Stellen and he placed his hands around my waist and I put my hands on his shoulders. We swayed a little to the music. I looked around to see if anyone was laughing at me but no one was even looking at us so I relaxed and actually started to enjoy it.

"You still hate me, don't you?" I looked up at him and he was shyly looking down at the floor. Eye contact was not his thing.

"I wouldn't say hate, but we are never, ever, ever getting back together." I said, quoting the Taylor Swift song. He didn't pick up on that but instead held me tighter and rested his chin on my head until the song was over. When it finished, we walked back to the table and sat down without speaking.

I looked around and noticed someone that I hadn't before. It was Sheriff Carmichael. He was wearing a suit. I wasn't used to seeing him out of uniform. He was sitting at a table across the room. When I finally approached the table, he looked up and didn't seem surprised.

"Sheriff, what are you doing here?"

"Well, I was invited, same as you. Freya, this is my wife, Michelle." I said hello to his wife, a pretty brunette in a black and white one shoulder maxi dress.

"What's going on in the investigation? Are you here tonight to keep an eye on me; is that why you're really here?"

"I can't talk about that now," he said looking sideways at his wife. "Now is not the place to discuss this." I felt embarrassed. He admonished me like a child.

"Okay, well, I guess you'll read about it in my new article. Bye." And I walked away with his mouth gaping. That'll fix him. When I got back to the table, Ali asked if I'd accompany her to the ladies room. We went, in a pair as women do and Desdemona followed us with Greta.

The bathroom was just as fancy as the dining room. The sinks were white and grey marble with brass fixtures. Floor to ceiling mirrors lined one wall. Black and white geometric floor tiles covered the floor. The ceiling, like the dining room was arched with mini brass chandeliers hanging every six feet. Matching pink and grey damask silk sofas were arranged in the far corner. Soft classical music was playing overhead.

Ali and I plopped down on one of the sofas and Greta and Desi, as she liked to be called, sat daintily on the other. We gossiped for a few minutes about what the other women were wearing. I asked Desi about her upcoming wedding and she was actually very nice. Not at all like I thought, she would be. We checked our makeup and visited for few minutes more before Greta and Desi left. Ali and I talked for a while longer.

"Are you coming? If we stay any longer, they'll probably come looking for us," she joked.

"Yeah, in a minute, I just want to check my messages."

Ali left and I was finally all alone. As much as I was enjoying the evening and the company, I'm used to being by myself. I checked my messages and read a couple from Keith and one from Enid. I texted Lorna about the restaurant and described what a beautiful place this would be to have a wedding reception, hoping she'd take the hint.

I checked my watch. I had been gone too long. I sniffed the air. Was that smoke? Maybe someone was smoking nearby. But it didn't smell like cigarette smoke or even pipe smoke. The smell was stronger near the door and when I tried to open it, it wouldn't open. It seemed locked and it was warm to the touch. There was no lock on this door, at least not from the inside anyway. I pushed and pushed but it wouldn't move. I banged on the door and yelled for a few minutes but no one could hear me.

Then it hit me, the bathrooms were in the back of the club. We had to walk quite a way from the main room to get here. Then I remembered what The FBI said about Lukas targeting me. Maybe he started a fire. I almost started to panic but I stopped myself. I took a deep breath and pulled out my phone but I saw that I had no bars. Damn it! I'd used up all my data. Are you kidding?

I heard fire trucks in the distance. Oh my God. The building must be on fire. Just like in my dream. Think! I looked out the window. It was facing the woods behind the golf course. There were so many trees, I couldn't see anything. Besides, it was dark now and the only light came from the white lights on the little tress below.

There was a balcony to the right of me. I wondered if I could reach it. I opened the window and the cold night air hit me full force in the face. I lost my breath from the shock of it. It must be at least zero. Great, all I had on was my silk dress. I looked down and the ground below was as least forty feet away. The fire trucks were getting closer. Maybe they could rescue me like they do in the movies. I could just wait here until the trucks arrived and scream until they heard me. But before I shut the window, dark smoke started to billow in from the hallway. It was thick and dark and had a chemical smell to it. I coughed immediately. My eyes began to water. I couldn't wait. I had to make my escape now.

I looked down again at the ground. I'd rather fall to my death than burn to death. I stuck my evening bag into the waist band of my panties and pulled up my dress and tied the silky material in a knot and slung one leg over the window sill and then the other. I crept over as carefully as I could on the skinny ledge and reached for the railing of the adjacent balcony. It was at least six feet away; too far to grip.

So, I leaned over as far as I could on one leg and reached until the railing was in my grasp. I grabbed hold and pulled myself toward it. I took my leg and jumped off the ledge and hopped over onto the balcony. I landed just barely before slipping off and hanging from the railing by both hands.

By now, the black smoke was billowing out of the bathroom window and I heard glass cracking and popping from the inside. I swung myself up and towards the balcony and got my leg hooked between the balcony railings. I pulled myself up onto the balcony using the wrought iron railing.

I'm so exhausted now and my lungs hurt from the cold air. I couldn't feel my fingers anymore. But I did it. I leaned over the railing and let myself fall onto the floor and rested there for a moment.

Miraculously, I heard voices and yelling below me. I crawled over and saw flashlights.

"Help, help; I'm up here," I screamed.

"Freya, is that you?" It was Stellen.

"Yes, get me down."

"Hold on. I'll get help."

I could barely see anything now; between the blackness of the evening sky and the smoke, I couldn't even see the lights below me anymore. I was having trouble breathing. I tried to stand and as I did, the glass shattered behind me and I fell forward onto my hands.

It was obvious I couldn't stay here and wait for help. I looked around and saw very faintly through the smoke, the shapes of dozens of pine trees. I remembered the last time I'd climbed a tree. I was twelve years old. Well, here goes. I swung one leg over the balcony and grabbed one of the branches. They were close enough to touch. So, I grabbed them with both hands and jumped off the balcony and as I did, large flames burst from the window engulfing the balcony, turning it into an inferno. I was hanging from the branches now and too tired to pull myself up and no longer able to feel my hands, I let myself fall.

CHAPTER THIRTY

"Freya, honey, wake up." The voice was familiar and I smiled to myself.

"Freya, you don't have much time, wake up now!" I opened my eyes and my mother was sitting beside me holding my hand.

"Mom, is that you?" She looked like she did when I was little. Short dark hair and no make-up; wearing jeans and a tee shirt- my mom was no nonsense.

"Is this a dream?" I asked.

"Does it matter? Dreams are nothing more than our subconscious telling us what we need to know. I'm here to help you, but I don't have much time. You need to wake up before the killer gets here. He's very close. He set the fire but you escaped."

"You are injured and the temperature is below zero. You're unconsciousness and you don't have any time left. Wake up now!"

I opened my eyes and the first thing I felt was not the cold but the fiery pain in my bad knee. I must have reinjured it in the fall. Then I remembered the fire

260

and the balcony. I looked up and realized that I was lying on the ground within a little grove of trees off from the building. I could hear screaming, yelling, and popping noises and glass breaking. I tried to sit up but it hurt too much. So, I start yelling.

"Help, I'm over here. I can't walk. Help! Somebody please help me!"

I could see a man coming toward me through the smoke. He kneeled down beside me. The next thing I felt was the sensation of blackness covering me. It felt like I was sliding down into a deep warm hole. I just wanted to sleep. I closed my eyes and surrendered to the darkness and warmth that oblivion offered.

"Is she okay?" I heard someone ask but I couldn't see anything. My eyes refused to open.

I could feel people touching me. My knee was now numb. I was unable to speak or move. It felt like being paralyzed but I didn't mind the loss of control. It was weird because I'm such a control freak sometimes. But right now, I didn't care about anything. Maybe this was heaven.

"We've given her a shot of tramadol. It'll help with the pain. She's out of it right now. We need to get her to the hospital for an x-ray of that knee. I'm sure the patella is fractured but if we get her immobilized and into a brace, she might not need surgery. As long as nothing is torn, she'll heal in a few weeks," said the EMT.

"I'll text her brother. Can I ride along with her? I'm her best friend."

"Sure, hop in."

"Don't worry Freya, I'm here with you." I felt Ali take my hand and that was the last thing I remembered.

When I did wake up, I found myself in the Emergency Department of Mercy Regional. I recognized some of the staff I worked with when I volunteered. The nurse explained my injury to me. Nothing was torn but there was a hairline fracture across the patella from my fall. Apparently, I was lucky. I was supposed to wear a brace and take it easy for a few weeks. As Ali left the room to call Jake, Sheriff Carmichael entered the room.

"You are either the luckiest person I've ever met or the unluckiest – I still haven't decided."

"What happened?" I asked.

Carmichael pulled up a chair and filled me in. A fire was set. Lukas was suspected but was still at large. They found his vehicle at Potters Mill. Apparently, he'd been hiding out there. But the good news, Caleb was cooperating with the authorities and was with the FBI right now. Apparently, his family wanted him to cut a deal.

"I'll talk with you tomorrow. We'll take your statement then. Take care of yourself."

After he left, Ali filled me in on what happened after I got locked in the bathroom. She was so dramatic; she should have been an actress. I laughed so much my knee started to hurt again. The meds must be wearing off now. Apparently, Stellen's dad was no hero. He was the first person out the door. Pushing and shoving the others around him. He even knocked down an elderly woman. That doesn't look very good for his campaign, I surmised.

"Can I go home now? Jake will be home in a couple hours. I really just want to go to bed in my own room. I don't want to stay overnight."

"Yeah, the nurse said you could be discharged any time, but there is someone here to see you first."

She opens the door and Stellen walked in. "Freya, are you okay? I'm so sorry this happened to you."

"It's not your fault." I said trying to sit up. Stellen adjusted the bed to an upright position and helped me to stand up. My brace was keeping my leg straight so it was hard to walk; but I managed to make my way over to the bath room and attempted to get dressed. My dress was ruined. I had nothing to wear.

Stellen laughed. "I thought of that. This is from someone named Rachel." He handed me a pair of sweats and a top. "She said you could borrow them."

Rachel, my friend from the Emergency Department; I'd have to thank her later. I dressed quickly and washed my face. Some of my hair was loose in the front, with strands falling around my face but the French braid was still secure, nonetheless. I'd have to wear the hospital slippers. I don't know where my heels were and frankly, I don't ever want to see them again. I'm back to sneakers and ankle boots after tonight.

I wrapped myself in my coat. Stellen grabbed it before he exited the restaurant. He really came through for me tonight. I realized how lucky I am as I snuggled into my warm wool coat. I checked my purse, which amazingly was sitting on the bedside table. The gun was still there, a lot of good that did me tonight. I should have brought a fire extinguisher.

I signed the discharge papers and told Ali that Stellen could give us both a ride but she's already called Lincoln to pick her up. As I waited for Stellen to bring his car around to the Emergency Department entrance, Lincoln showed up and Ali got in his car and waved to me through the glass as they drove away. She gave me the thumbs up signal that we used as kids. I smiled at the memory. Stellen soon arrived and we left for home.

I called Jake and filled him in. He and Lorna had gone to New Haven but there was a detour due to a tractor trailer truck accident on the highway. He'd try to be home in a couple hours. The police had surveillance outside our house just in case Lukas came back. But I'm sure he's long gone by now. All I wanted to do was take a bath and go to sleep. I reeked of smoke and I'm covered in soot.

My brother told me he loved me. I'm overcome. The last time he told me that was when our parents had been killed. He wasn't verbal like that but I knew he loved me just the same. But, it was still great to hear the words. I said it back to him.

Stellen and I drove the rest of the way in silence. After he parked in front of my house, he dashed over to my side of the car and helped me walk into the house. He very gently sat me down on the couch in the living room. I could see the police car from the front window.

"I can stay until Jake gets here." Stellen offered.

I almost took him up on his offer but I wanted to be independent; in spite of everything that had happened tonight. I thanked him and gave him a hug and a kiss on the cheek. I promised to call him tomorrow. But right now, I just needed rest and some alone time.

I went into the bathroom and started filling the tub with all the bath salts I had on hand. I stripped off my clothes and wrapped myself in a towel. I dropped everything I'd been wearing into the washing machine and added double the amount of soap. I turned on the Christmas tree and tossed my no longer beautiful dress into the trash. It was torn and smelled like smoke.

Then I returned to my bath and got into the now filled tub of fragrant water smelling of every scent I owned – lilac, jasmine, honeysuckle, and pear. If that didn't mask the stench of smoke then nothing, wood. I put a wash cloth over my face and closed my eyes.

An hour later I emerged from the bath with clean skin, clean hair and no trace of the evening's conflagration left. I dressed in my usual Yankees nightshirt and navy sweats with thick plushy socks.

Suddenly, I was ravenous so I scurried into the kitchen to see what I could rustle up. It was almost impossible to walk fast with this brace but I did my best. As I entered the kitchen, I didn't bother to flick on the lights. I knew the layout in the dark.

I pulled out a strawberry pop tart and stuck in the toaster. As I turned around, I could see almost faintly, in the door of my chrome refrigerator, the shadow of a person standing behind me. That's when I realized, I wasn't alone.

CHAPTER THIRTY-ONE

"I've wanted to meet you for a long time. Now, we're finally face to face. I must say, you do have the prettiest hazel-green eyes I've ever seen. Oh, does that make you uncomfortable? Are you one of those women who can't take a compliment from a man?"

It was Lukas Trott, right here in my kitchen. He looked like Caleb but a little different. His eyes seemed darker and features less open and friendly. Of course, the guy was a killer so maybe I was biased.

"I feel like I already know you Freya. I've been watching you for a while now. And I've read all your articles- every word. It's hard to believe you never met Joey. You kind of remind me of her, young, pretty, confident, – way too confident."

"Did you set the fire?" I asked.

"You know I did."

"Did you kill Joey?"

"You know I did."

"Why did you do it?"

"Why does anyone do anything; because they can? Look, we had a plan and she was going to ruin it. She had to go."

"You were seen in Boston."

"Yeah, well, I was there, but I came back here. I wanted to see you in the flesh." As he said this, he took his thumb and ran it down the side of my face. He stepped closer to me. He inhaled.

"Mmm, you smell good." I automatically stepped back and he pressed me up against the cold refrigerator door. He placed his hand on my breast through my nightshirt and squeezed. I winced and he smiled. "Are you a virgin, Freya?"

"No, I'm not and the police are right outside. Just one scream from me and they're here in a flash."

He shook his head. "No, they're not going to save you tonight. It's kind of hard to play hero when your neck has been cut. Piano wire does that to a person."

"That's how you killed Quentin." I said trying to buy some time.

"Yeah, that old man had a big mouth, he had to go too." He removed his hand from my face and reached up under my shirt. He tried to pull down my sweats. He pushed himself against me and I felt his hardness. Oh my God, he's going to rape me. Think.

"Lukas, can I please sit down? My knee is killing me. I broke my patella tonight when I fell."

I said this as sweetly as I could. He was taken off guard by my question. He backed up and let me hop over to the sofa to sit down. I was trying to stall. I needed to get to my bedroom. The gun was still in my purse. I couldn't out run him. He followed me into the living room and noticed the six foot Christmas tree and the presents piled beneath it. He walked over to the tree and looked out the front window. It was dark out with only the street light visible.

Then I saw it, the scissors I was using this morning. I was wrapping gifts. They were partially hidden under the wrapping paper. Lukas was now looking at the childhood photos of Jake and me on the wall. I carefully extended my hand over to the coffee table, my hand hovering over the scissors. I glanced over at Lukas; he was still studying the pictures, so I grabbed hold of the scissors and slid them towards me, never taking my eyes off of him. I hid them under me as I conspicuously readjusted the pillows under my leg. I lay back on the couch with the scissors under me. He turned to me then.

"So, Freya, what am I going to do with you? I tried to burn you, but that didn't work. How do I stop you?"

Acting braver than I felt I answered him. "I have an idea. You leave; go far away and never come back here. You can go to Venezuela. There's no extradition there. The evidence against you is circumstantial at best. Or, you can stay here and fight this thing, "I said calmly.

"Your family is rich. All you need is a good lawyer and that takes money; you've got that. You know that rich people don't go to jail." I said this confidently. I took my time. Maybe, if I could keep him talking, Jake would get home, see the dead police officer out front, and call for help. Or, Jake would get home and the distraction would give me enough time to act. I knew if I had to, I could kill Lukas. I could feel the hard outline of the scissors beneath me.

"Venezuela? I've always liked warm weather. You'll call the police as soon as I leave, won't you?"

"Not if you tie me up. I can't run so that's not an option for me."

He was thinking about it, he was actually thinking about it. I could see his eyes flicker back and forth. I learned from my Psychology course that you could tell everything you need to know about a person's thought process through their eye movements.

"I like you Freya. I even admire you but I don't trust you. I don't trust any women. You're all the same. You're all liars and con artists. Well, I'm not stupid."

My heart skipped a beat. He suddenly stood up and quickly walked over to me. I couldn't think. The sudden knocking at the front door stunned us both. We look at it, in unison. Lukas puts his fingers to his lips.

The knocking continued and got louder and more urgent. Then, the knocking turned to banging.

"Freya, I know you're in there. Are you okay? Jake called me. He wants me to check on you. Let me in." It was Erik.

"I know you're still mad at me but please let me in. I'm worried about you."

"You'd better leave now, Lukas." I whispered. I reached under the pillow and grabbed the scissors. Lukas was standing directly over me concentrating on the door so I pulled out my hand and drove one of the three inch blades as deeply, as I could, into the upper thigh of his left leg. He screamed and doubled over almost on top of me.

"Erik, Lukas is in here, help!"

Erik burst in as Lukas pulled the scissors out from his leg and thrust it towards me. I took my good leg and kicked him as hard as I could in his crotch, sending him backwards over the coffee table and hitting his head on the floor, knocking him unconscious. Erik sprinted over and grabbed the scissors from the floor. He checked Lukas – he was unconscious.

"Do you have any rope?" he asked me.

I rushed into the kitchen and grabbed the leftover twine I was using that morning to tie Christmas lights to my porch railing. Erik and I turned Lukas over onto his stomach and tied his hands and

271

feet behind him. The wound in his leg was bleeding copiously all over my hard wood floor so I grabbed an old towel to staunch the blood flow. I called 911 and then Agent Bent's number and left a message for her. Erik and I sat and waited for the police. We collapsed onto the sofa. I rested my head on his shoulder and he put his arm around me.

"So, I guess this means you're no longer mad at me anymore?" he mused.

"Oh no, I'm still pissed at you for not telling me about your girlfriend back home, but I'm happy you're here now."

I kissed him on the lips and we sat like that, in silence until we heard the police sirens coming closer and closer to my home.

CHAPTER THIRTY-TWO

By time the police and FBI arrived, Lukas was conscious. He didn't say anything. They read his Miranda warning, but he was staring straight at me from across the room. I couldn't read his mind but his look told me he hated me and frankly, my dear, I don't give a damn.

The police had a hard time getting him to stand up with all the twine we tied around him, so they had to cut it off. The sheriff gave me one of his looks that I'd grown accustomed to lately. I could tell he was pleased but he said nothing.

My knee was aching again so I swallowed a couple painkillers. I'd have to call Dr. Taggart about a steroid injection. He was the surgeon who fixed my knee last time it was injured.

The pain wasn't the same as when I shattered my knee a couple years back and tore my meniscus; but it was bad. I hobbled off to my room to get dressed. The police wanted my statement and honestly, I just wanted to get this over. I heard Jake's truck in the driveway and quickly shut my bedroom door. Let

Erik update him. I was in no mood for an inquisition right now.

When I finally emerged from my room, dressed in a heavy sweater and jeans, Jake was standing by the couch looking down at the congealed puddle of blood left there. When he saw me, he did the unthinkable. He ran over and grabbed me so hard; he lifted me up off the floor. He held me like for a few moments and tears sprang to my eyes. I swear; he'd aged overnight. Lorna hugged me too and I heard yapping sound at my feet. It was her little dog. I laughed in spite of the earlier horrific events of the evening and hugged them both.

"Honey, are you okay? Can I do anything for you?" asked Lorna looking at me; her expression showing both shock and concern.

My leg was in brace, my face flushed, and my hair, half blow dried was crimping up the way it does if I don't use an anti-frizzing serum. No make-up and dark circles under my eyes told the truth. I looked like hell because I'd been through hell.

"I'm going to the police station to give a statement. Don't wait up for me."

I walked past them and out the front door and got into the FBI vehicle with Agents Bent and Mooney. Erik was standing on my porch talking to an officer. He gave me a smile and a wink. He was meeting me at the station a little later.

We drove through town and all the festivity of the Christmas season. It was early morning now and the downtown was vacant. Everyone was home in bed, safe and warm, everyone except me.

We parked and I started to walk as carefully as I could over the fresh snow covering the sheet of ice beneath it. All I needed right now was to fall and hurt my other knee. As if reading my mind, Agent Mooney took my hand and helped me to the side door of the police station. A private entrance; we walked down a hallway and into a spacious new office and I took a seat across from them at a large square oak table.

"Freya, we're going to wait for the sheriff, he should be here shortly. Would you like a cup of coffee or a glass of water?" Agent Bent asked me. And for a moment, she sounded more like a mom than an FBI special agent did. I said yes to the water.

During the three hour interview, I learned quite a few things. First, Lukas was in Boston but came back and was hiding out at the abandoned Potters' Mill. The police found camping gear and food on the second level of the structure and enough gasoline to start a huge fire. I wasn't surprised since he already admitted to me that he did it.

I also learned that Caleb was offered a plea deal since he cooperated. But the police wouldn't tell me anything about that. It was brother against brother now. I wondered which would win.

"You ready?" Erik asked. "I'm looking forward to some of Polly's famous pancakes, how about you?"

"I'm more of a French toast girl, myself. But let's get out of here."

By time we arrived at Polly's Diner, it was busy with the morning rush, we chose a booth in the back of the diner facing the wall. While we waited for our food, we checked our phones for incoming messages or texts. What did people do before cell phones? Soon, our food arrived.

"Well, fancy meeting you here."

I turned around to see Les Murry from the Beacon. He was dressed in running clothes. Les loved physical activity and ran rain or shine, snow or no snow.

I kidded him about it. "How can you run in weather like this? There's snow on the ground, aren't you afraid you'll fall and break something?"

"Me? I'm a former professional athlete. I know what I'm doing." He laughed. "Do you mind if I sit down?" Les sat anyway, before I could give him an answer.

"Freya, I'd like to interview you for the paper. I just heard from the police department that Lukas Trott attacked you in your home last night and tried to burn you to death in the country club fire. Is that all true?"

"Yeah," I said simply.

For the next hour, I told my side of the story and Erik interjected his part as well. Les took notes as I meticulously explained my escape from the Canterbury Club balcony. I left out the part about my mother's ghost helping me wake up. I'm sure that Les didn't believe in ghosts and at this point, I was wondering if it was all just another intuitive dream, as the Salem Medium called them.

He stood up and shook our hands. The article would be in tomorrow's paper. As we were walking out of the diner, my cell rang. It was Ben. He wanted me to come over to his house. It was very important. So, Erik and I drove over and arrived a little after 9:00. I was wide awake, even though I never slept last night.

Ben answered the door and I was surprised to see that Jon was also there with little Biscuit. Jon explained that he was now living at Ben's house. Since both were alone and without family, they decided that, they should try being roommates. Ben's house was so large; they'd have their own space and independence. Jon had applied to the police academy and was waiting to hear from them. We sat in the large but still sparsely decorated living room. Ben handed me an envelope.

"Do you want me to open this?"

"Yes, I do," he said.

I tore open the envelope to reveal a legal document. I scanned it quickly, reading the words.

"What is this?" I asked.

"My Uncle died yesterday and he wanted me to give you this after he was gone. He wanted you to read it," said Ben.

It was a letter addressed to me and was dated yesterday. I read it out loud so Erik can hear.

Dear Freya,

I'm dictating this letter to my attorney. I'm not long for this world so it's important that I do this now. I'm relieved that the truth is finally out. I want everyone to know that Oliver Jon Keating is my relative.

I am dividing the entire Putnam-Ingersoll estate between Benjamin and Jon. I trust that they will invest and spend it wisely. I also want to bequeath you something for all your hard work and dogged determination. In my day, women had babies and stayed home to raise them but things are different now and you are a prime example of what a woman is capable of accomplishing. That's why I'm leaving you the sum of $250,000. Pay off your tuition, buy a sports car, or open a detective agency; the future is yours. My advice; be wise and be prudent but never give up on your dreams or your goals.

All my best,

Judge Maurice Anthony Pringle

"Ben, this is too much, I can't accept this." I said handing back the letter.

278

"Oh yes you will and there's more. Jon and I wanted to do something special to thank you." Ben handed me another piece of paper. It was a proposal to the Claremont College Board of Directors, for a journalism scholarship to be awarded every year to a deserving student to study journalism. And the name is- the Freya Barrett Journalism Scholarship.

I handed the letter to Erik. He read it and smiled at me. "Well, now what?"

"I need to make a phone call." With tears in my eyes, I walked into Ben's kitchen and hit speed dial on my cell phone. A voice said hello.

"Emily? Hi, it's Freya. I have some good news for you. Is your mom there? I need to tell you both something."

CHAPTER THIRTY-THREE

A week has passed since my knee injury. I've been going to the Evergreen Orthopedic Clinic for physical therapy. Dr. Taggart was giving me an arthrocentesis today to alleviate the swelling and pain in my knee. It's healing but just not as fast as it should. I'm still wearing my brace. But, if everything goes well, I should be okay in about four to six weeks. Jake offered to drive me to my appointment a little later.

Christmas was in a few days and amazingly most things had returned to normal. Lorna moved back into her house. Jake's ribs are almost healed and the Sentinel and Beacon have both printed articles about the arrest of the Trott brothers and their link to the recent murders in Agatha Falls.

My article was featured in the Beacon with my firsthand account of my escape from the fire and Lukas Trott's attack in my home. I'd become a regular celebrity around here.

"Hey Freya, are you ready? I'd like to leave a bit early since more snow is expected."

"Sure, I'm ready."

I grabbed my bag and hobbled out the door, leaning on Jake as I walked down the driveway to his truck. He helped me up into it and I winced as a searing pain ran around the perimeter of my knee and shot down my leg. He buckled me in and we drove off toward the clinic. I still hadn't told Jake about seeing our mother at the fire.

"Jake, I need to tell you something. And I don't know how you'll take it, so just listen okay?" He glanced over at me with that worried look he got sometimes.

"No, it's nothing bad, I'm fine but something happened at the fire last week and I wanted you to know about it. I've been waiting for the right moment to tell you."

"After I fell, I must have been knocked out. I heard a voice in my head telling me to wake up and warning me that I didn't have a lot of time. Eventually I opened my eyes and guess who I dreamed I saw?"

"Mom," he said deadpan.

"How did you know that?"

"I saw her too, after my truck accident last month. After I hit the tree, my truck caught fire. I was unconscious. Anyway, I heard a voice telling me to get out. When I did come to, I swear, she was sitting beside me holding my hand and she was wearing that t-shirt she always wore, the tie die with the peace symbol. Do you remember that shirt?"

I nodded, remembering it fondly. It was her weekend shirt. Tired of wearing suits during the week to her classes, she took to casual wear on the weekends.

"I didn't know your truck caught fire. You never said."

"No, I didn't want to worry you. I woke up and pulled the extinguisher from the back of the truck. I put it out but just in time or the whole thing would have probably exploded. Anyway I saw her too and it didn't feel like a dream at all, at least not at the time."

I relay my conversation with the Salem Medium to him and he listened without interruption.

"Do you think it was her ghost?"

"I don't know about paranormal or supernatural stuff, I'm not a big believer in that. But there is one thing I know about. And that's the power of a mother's love for her children. I don't think even death can stop that," said Jake bluntly.

He parked in front of the clinic and I sat there for a minute just absorbing what he had just said. He took my hand and squeezed it.

"Do you want me to wait for you; because, if you don't, I've got Christmas shopping to finish."

I told him I'd call him when I was ready and slid out of the truck as gently as I could and walked carefully into the clinic. I checked in, took a seat, and waited.

Evergreen Orthopedic Clinic was on the outskirts of Agatha Falls, almost on the border of Pine Haven, our closest town. Secluded, it was surrounded by the Old North Woods and was owned and operated by Dr. Lyle Taggart and Dr. Beverly Gleason, both orthopedic specialists. Dr. Taggart performed my knee surgery a couple years back and he was a transplant from Chicago too. The waiting area was busy, like it normally was this time of year. The waiting room was filled with patients in casts and splints.

"Freya? Would you come this way?" said Jade. She was a young nurse who worked for Dr. Taggart. She led me down the hallway toward the back of the clinic and into one of the patient rooms.

"We're running about fifteen minutes behind. So, grab a magazine, and Dr. Taggart will be in shortly."

She left, shutting the door behind her. I grabbed one of the magazines from the rack and began to read an article about an overhyped young actress that I wasn't crazy about.

I didn't have any interest in celebrities' lives. I'd rather spend my time living my own life than reading about someone else's. A short time later, I heard a knock on the door.

"Come in." I said

Dr. Taggart smiled when he saw me. A tall man with a lanky build; he was in his early forties, married with three young children. He was funny, relaxed, and very approachable. He took the magazine from me.

"I think she's overrated, don't you? I saw her last movie. It wasn't very good." We bantered for a few minutes about my life and my plans for the upcoming holiday. Then he removed my brace and examined my knee.

"You have fluid buildup in your knee and that inflammation is causing your pain. This is your Prepatellar bursa. It's a small fluid filled sac in front of your knee. It acts like a cushion and reduces the friction between the pressure points in your knee, like your tendons, muscles, and joints. It's been damaged from your fall."

"A corticosteroid injection will fix that but first we have to drain the fluid. That's called an arthrocentesis. So, Jade and I will get you prepped for that but first, I need to apologize for a slight delay. I have to make a very important phone call and then we will take care of you. Is that all right? It shouldn't be more than a ten minute wait."

"That's fine."

"Why don't you lay back and take a rest. Jade will be in shortly."

He left and a few minutes later, Jade entered with a tray covered with medical instruments and placed it on the table beside me.

284

"Dr. Taggart will be in soon." She left and I continued to lie down on the medical exam table with my knee elevated on a couple pillows. I closed my eyes. I must have dropped off. I hadn't been sleeping well this past week.

When I did wake up, it was dark and I almost forgot where I was. It took me a few seconds before I realized I was still at the orthopedic clinic waiting for an injection.

I suddenly became super alert and somehow I knew I wasn't alone in the room. I thought I could faintly hear breathing. I turned my head slightly to my left and then, all at once, I lost my breath entirely. Something was thrown over my head; covering my entire face. I couldn't breathe. My hands immediately went to my face and I pulled at the piece of cloth.

I panicked and thrashed my legs, kicking out blindly. Then, I heard something fall over. The pressure on the cloth lessened slightly and I was able to take a small breath but it was enough air to rejuvenate me.

I fought for my life. I felt my left fist strike out and hit flesh and the bag fell; freeing me to sit up. I gulped fresh air but it was still dark and I couldn't see very clearly. I jumped off the table wincing at the searing pain in my knee. Then the room was flooded with light.

"You rotten bitch!" the voice said.

I looked at the person standing in front of me and it took a moment to register who was standing there. It would be an understatement to say that I was stunned. But it all made sense now. I saw the connection between Joey, Quentin, and especially Sheriff Pringle; the airport expansion and probably the death of Eloise Pringle. Now I got it, it was all about the money.

"So, you're not a victim of foul play after all, are you Juanita?" I asked.

"You little bitch. You spoiled everting. And, now my Uncle has split the entire inheritance between Ben and this kid from Arizona. Who the hell is he? He just shows up, out of the blue and we're all supposed to kiss his ass because 200 years ago somebody had an affair."

"Not just anybody. Agatha Putnam, the founder of this town. Is that why you did all this, for the money?" I said quietly as I looked around the room for a weapon to use in my defense. Juanita was a holding a scalpel and by the look of her, she wasn't afraid to use it on me. I needed to stall. I needed to keep her talking.

"How did you do it? I never even suspected you," I said hoping my flattery would buy me enough time to think of a way out of this.

She sneered, "My aunt just wouldn't die. She was over 90 years old and she wouldn't die. She had all that money in the bank and she wouldn't give it to us until her death, so I helped her along."

"What did you do?"

"I waited one night when no one was around, and went to her hospital bed after visiting hours. I took a pillow and I covered her face with it. She was asleep and never woke up. I did her a kindness," she said with a smirk.

"Joey saw you," I said softly.

"I don't know how she did, I was so careful. But she told Caleb. He couldn't control her so I had Luke put her down," she said businesslike.

"How did you meet Lukas?"

"Where else do you meet a guy, at a bar? He was in town visiting his brother. We had a great summer and he was getting ready to go back to Colorado but I came up with the plan and he helped me. Caleb got brought in at the end, when Joey told him what happened."

"What about Quentin?"

"He had a big mouth and I hated his family for what they did to us over the years. He had it coming." She said this all very offhanded.

"Did your brother have it coming? You killed him too," I said boldly.

She shook her head wearily. "Linus wouldn't cooperate. When he found out what I was planning, he tried to talk me out of it. He and Luke were arguing and Luke pushed him and he fell. That was an accident. I regret that. But I won't regret shutting you up. Every day another article in the paper, who do you think you are, hmmm? Do you really think that anyone would believe you anyway?"

"Well, if I'm not a threat, then why did Lukas try to kill me and why are you here now?"

If looks could kill, her expression was stone cold, "because I earned that money! I did everything they asked of me and what did I get for it in the end, nothing. Always the men in the family, they got everything. Women were second class citizens in my family, "she said bitterly.

She continued as if she were talking to herself, "You got married, you had babies, and you kept quiet. Well, I wouldn't. My father used to have sex with me. Did you know that? It started when I was eight years old. Yeah, and Linus knew and did nothing. My mother knew and she did nothing either" Now I remember what the judge said about Linus being too close to Juanita. How had he gotten it so wrong?

"My mother was a mouse and she ignored me. No one cared. And my great Aunt Eloise blamed me. No one tried to protect me. They just acted as if it never happened. They ignored it and they ignored me. So, as I see it, I earned that money!"

Her eyes were so hard. They held no warmth. Her posture was rigid and her hand strained as she squeezed the scalpel even tighter. If I didn't do something soon, she was going to kill me. I needed to

288

try and defuse her anger. I knew from my psychology class that if someone was angry, you could try to deflate it by validating it and apologizing to them. I had nothing left to lose.

"I'm sorry that happened to you, Juanita. Someone should have stood up for you." She looked at me then, a little softness entered her eyes. "I don't blame you for feeling this way. I would too." She continued to stand there, just looking at me. So, I changed the subject.

"Where's Jade and Dr. Taggart? What have you done with them?"

"They're tied up on the closet with the rest of the staff. I told the patients to go home, that there was some sort of emergency."

"Why don't you just leave now and run away? I won't say anything."

"No, I'm not leaving here until I got what I came for," she said as she lunged toward me, cutting my arm with the scalpel. I put my arms up to cover my face. I just happened to look down and that's when I saw it on the floor, a few inches from my left foot. I dragged it under me and stood in front of it. I quickly kneeled down over it and rubbed my knee. Thankful that I was good at play acting, I gave it a shot. I had nothing to lose.

"Please Juanita, don't kill me. We can work out a deal. I have money now, you can have it."

She looked at me with interest as I picked up the weapon with my right hand and held it behind me. I kept talking.

"Your uncle left me $250,000. You can have it, if you let me live. Drive me to the bank and I'll sign it over to you. Then, you can leave here and start your life over someplace else. You're still young. You have your whole life ahead of you."

Her eyes left my face for just a second while she considered my offer, but that was all the time I needed as I thrust the needle into her neck. But I misjudged my aim and instead hit her directly in her left eye. Screaming, she dropped the scalpel and covered her face with her hands and I ran as fast as I could down the hall and out the front door.

A car driving past saw me attempting to flag it down and stopped. I told them to call the police. There was a crazy woman inside the clinic and she had the medical staff tied up. The driver looked at me as if I was crazy but they believed me and called 911.

I sat in the car and waited for the police to arrive and sure enough, Sheriff Carmichael, Deputy Mott and two police cars showed up and ran inside. Within minutes, Juanita was led to the police car in handcuffs, her eyes covered with a bandage.

I got out of the car then and just stood there for a moment watching her led off to her impending punishment, a life in prison, most likely. But, when I thought about her childhood and everything she'd told me, I felt a little sorry for the little girl she used to be and wondered what kind of woman she could have become if someone had loved her enough to protect her. Now, we'll never know.

CHAPTER THIRTY-FOUR

"I want to show you my special place. " Erik raised one eyebrow. "You already showed me that last night." He joked as he kissed my shoulder and rolled over in bed to face me.

"No, you moron, it's a place I used to go to when I was a kid. It used to mean a lot to me and I want to share it with you. Get dressed. I'll take you there."

I jumped out of bed, wrapping the sheet around me toga style. I rushed across the hall to the newly renovated bathroom for a quick shower. When I showed up last night at Erik's house, I didn't think we'd end up in bed. I wanted to show him that my knee healed and now we could go cross country skiing together. But after I got here, we spent a long time talking and suddenly it just happened.

I know how that sounds. Maybe it was the relief that Lukas Trott was going to trial in a few months for the murders of Joey Taylor, Quentin Ambrose, and Linus Hadley and the attempt on my life, not to mention the fire he set. Juanita was also being tried separately for the murder of Eloise Putnam-Pringle and attempted murder. Caleb made a deal with the authorities and will face trial but on lesser charges.

Erik was glad to see that Lukas will spend the rest of his life in prison even though he wasn't convicted of Jacqueline's death. He was willing to settle. So, he's staying in Agatha Falls and working on a renovation of Potter's Mills. A company from Pennsylvania bought it and was thinking of turning into condo units. Jake and I had a bet as to how long this would last before it went kaput. This was the fourth time someone bought the mill and tried to renovate it.

It was late March now and we had a new mayor – Nat Baldwin trounced Stellen's dad in the election. I guess it didn't help your political image to knock people down as you're running out of a burning building.

Ben was elected to the city council and was working closely with them to ensure the fifty acres of land originally intended for the New England cotton tailed rabbit was established as an animal sanctuary. Jon was accepted into the Connecticut Police Academy. He's moving to Meriden to complete the 22 week course and then sit for the exam.

And me, well, I'm still writing for the college paper but I now have a weekly series in the local city paper; and I'm paid for it too. I focused on crime. Cold cases were my new passion. I no longer worked at the Coffee Shoppe but stopped by often to visit my old friends there.

Jake won the bid for the renovations at the Regency Hotel. He and Lorna were still together and we all had dinner together once a week. As far as the money, left to me by Judge Pringle, most if it I invested but I kept some of it. I haven't decided yet what I'm going to do with it. We dressed quickly and walked outside to enjoy a mild but crisp day.

"Where are we going?" asked Erik.

"It's a surprise." I said. We walked up my street and into my backyard and continued walking until we came to our final destination – the falls. We walked the 165 foot embankment together. The ground was wet and muddy and we slipped a few times. It wasn't so easy to get our footing. But we reached the top. When we arrived at the river's edge at the drop off, I walked across and Erik followed me holding my hand. We took our time with the sun directly overhead we had a lovely view of the valley below us.

"I used to do this when I first moved here. I was twelve years old and had no friends except for a neighborhood girl and we did it all summer long. I almost went over the side once and that was the last time I crossed- until today."

I reflected on all that had happened over the last few months. I walked down the hill toward my home with Erik behind me. When we reached my house, Jake was just walking in the back door.

"Hey, Freya, CPI is coming tonight. Are you ready for your ghost hunt?"

Jake teased me but since he'd taken over the renovations at the hotel, he'd noticed some creepy things going on there. Equipment going missing;

things being moved and strange noises that couldn't be accounted for seemed to be the norm since his crew showed up last week. One of his guys said he felt a hand on his shoulder but when he turned around, there was no one there.

Tobias Fairchild was the lead investigator for the Connecticut Paranormal Investigators or CPI as their known. His brother, Adam was filming the hunt for a film he was making on the subject. They agreed to let me tag along as an investigator in training and write about it for the Sentinel and the Beacon.

I've spent the last couple weeks getting all the equipment I needed for tonight - a flashlight, an EMF reader to detect electromagnetic fields, a motion sensor, a digital thermometer and a thermal imaging camera. The more advanced equipment will be used by the senior team members. I needed to be there by 10pm tonight. In the meantime, I started dinner.

Erik's been having dinner at my house almost every night. I liked having him and Jake home for dinner. And now that I no longer work nights at the restaurant, I have my evenings at home. My classes were during the day and I worked for the paper from home. I only go to the Beacon's office once a week so everything has worked out really well.

Erik and I had a long talk and he told me about his ex-girlfriend that he broke up with before he moved here last fall. He blamed my age for his reticence to get involved with me. But we both were willing to take a chance so we we're taking it day by day. Things between us were complicated but good.

295

After dinner, Jake retired to his office and Erik went home, leaving me time to dress for tonight. My uniform consisted of navy blue overalls that do nothing to enhance my figure. A tool belt around my waist to hold my equipment and a white cap that reads CPI is big red letters. It was almost 10pm as I parked in the back lot of the hotel; I saw several other people standing around and three large white vans with CPI on the side door.

A tall man with a red bushy hair walked briskly toward me. It was Tobias. "Hey Freya; glad to see you didn't back out." Noticing the look on my face, he explained himself. "I mean, sometimes people start to think about what could happen and they get scared. I'm glad you're not a scaredy cat."

"No, Tobias – I don't scare easy." I said.

"Good, let's get started."

An hour later and the team were ready to begin the investigation. The technicians had to set up cameras in key areas that were considered hot spots. These areas had previous paranormal episodes. So, I along with another tech had arranged cameras on the entire first floor of the hotel, including the lobby, the back office, the front parlor, the back sitting room and the kitchen and restaurant. A make shift command center was located in a van parked in the back lot.

There were ten of us in all, three technicians, two lead investigators, three junior investigators, and two cameramen. I had the distinction of being the only woman beside Crystal, Tobias's girlfriend but the group was young, friendly and the atmosphere was collegial in nature.

The second area being monitored was the basement. Supposedly, nobody liked to be down there alone. A women's voice and the crying of a baby had reportedly been heard by hotel staff. So, the senior investigators were covering that area. There was a lot of history to this building and I did extensive research before agreeing to sign on as an investigator. I wanted to make sure there was a story here. And there was.

The Regency Hotel was originally used as part of the Underground Railroad when it belonged to Seymour Lewis, a prominent local citizen and abolitionist in Agatha Falls. After his death in 1865, his son, Gideon sold the property to a wealthy retired lawyer from Boston who turned the spacious home into a thirteen room hotel.

The property was expanded twice, once in the 1920's with the addition of the adjoining building. This was converted into a kitchen and restaurant; and in 2008, the hotel purchased the other adjacent building, which added an additional twelve rooms. This current renovation will be the most extensive and Tobias and his team believed this was what unearthed the spectral visions, cold spots, smells, and sounds that now occurred more than ever. He explained that spirits sometimes get upset when their space was disturbed.

I called Nancy Johnson, the Salem Medium and filled her in on the CPI team. She would have loved to participate with the investigation but she was busy

297

helping with a kidnapping in Boston. So, Tobias was having another psychic take part tonight.

Edith Everett was a local psychic who came out of retirement for this evening only. She was 81 and her health was failing but she wanted to do one more reading at this hotel. She originally visited the hotel about ten years ago on Halloween. She made contact with several spirits who had passed over well before the hotel was established. Most of them were family members of the Lewis clan. So, she was excited about doing another reading tonight. Edith arrived at midnight- the witching hour.

"Okay, Freya, we're ready to begin our portion of the investigation. I want you and Pete to take EMF recordings in the kitchen and restaurant area first, and then make your way through the hotel until you reach the front lobby. Pete will be filming the event so ask the questions naturally, the way I showed you and you should be fine. If at any time, you start to feel sick or anxious, let Pete know. Novice investigators sometimes experience that when they start out."

"No problem."

He was right. Sometimes people who were new to paranormal investigations became sick or felt anxious or even depressed during a spiritual encounter. The spirit or entity can zap your energy and make you feel exhausted afterward. The building was totally dark with the exception of some flood lights and the emergency fire door exits. I could still see well enough to make my way toward the back of the building with Pete following me. I stood next to a window and checked my EMF recorder. Nothing was registering yet. The thermometer was giving me a temperature of 68 degrees. During paranormal contact, the temperature will drop due to the spirit siphoning off the heat for energy.

I began by asking questions of the spirit. First, I introduced myself and held out my tape recorder to record any voices.

"Hello, my name is Freya and I'd like to talk to the spirits of whoever is residing at this hotel. This is my friend Pete and we are not here to disturb you. We simply want to get to know you."

I said all this slowly and softly but in a natural speaking voice. I remembered what the Salem Medium said about spirits who've passed over, many didn't know they were dead and they were often lonely. They merely wanted to communicate with the living. I was hoping these spirts were friendly and wanted to talk.

"Can you tell me what your name is? And why you are here?"

I looked at my EMF recorder - nothing. No change in temp either so I moved closer to the kitchen island in the center of the gigantic kitchen. Surprisingly, this kitchen was totally modern for an 1865 building. This had always been the most modern part of the hotel and had several mini remodels over the years to keep it current.

"I understand that you have tried to communicate with kitchen staff recently by breaking glasses and speaking. Can you do that now? Can you send me a sign that you are here?" I shone my flashlight toward the pantry and for a second I think I saw something move.

"Pete, the pantry, did you see that? It looked like something just passed by really quickly."

"I'll walk over and film there. Follow behind me and keep talking." He said as he walked toward the darkened corner. I shivered and checked my thermometer. The temp had dropped to 58 degrees since the last time I checked it.

"Freya, prepare yourself, something might happen very soon. What, I don't know but something." He responded.

I continued asking questions when suddenly out of the corner of my eye; I saw the wall calendar to the right of me swinging back and forth on its hook.

"Pete, the calendar, check it out." I whispered.

"Yeah, I'm getting it." He said excitedly. "Keep talking. They like you."

"Oh, okay, hi, it's me Freya again. Can you tell me about yourself? How old are you? Can you tell me your name?" Just then, I heard a sound like a voice but garbled. So, I asked again, "Tell me your name."

"SAARAAA", said the voice.

I gasped and grabbed Pete's arm. "Did you hear that?" I asked excitedly.

But before he could reply, I heard glass breaking. Pete pointed the camera toward the noise. There was glass on the floor in front of us. But there were no glasses in sight.

"Where did that come from?" I asked Pete.

He shook his head. So, we walked around the perimeter of the kitchen and in the far corner stood a small table covered in juice glasses; at least 30 feet away from us. How the heck did that get all the way over here? Pete was still filming so I checked the EMF recorder again. It was going crazy now.

"Pete, check this out." I showed him the results. He nodded and we walked into the restaurant. The temperature was now 55 degrees. I was glad to be wearing gloves. It was cold in here now. My walkie-talkie squeaked and I jumped at the suddenness of it.

"Freya, are you there? This is Tobias. Please respond." I quickly told him about the last few minutes in the kitchen.

He and his tech were now in the basement of the hotel directly under the kitchen and restaurant where Pete and I were now standing. He asked me to put my EMF recorder on the floor in the center of the room. When I placed it there, it started to go crazy.

"Tobias, it's really off the charts now."

"Okay, keep it there and check it periodically. We just saw something wiz past us down here. I've got to investigate. Oh, and Freya, Edith is doing a reading in the upstairs bedroom where most of the psychic activity occurs. When you're done with the first floor, go to room 206." I agreed and signed off.

Pete and I walked around the perimeter of the restaurant but we were not picking up anything. The temperature had stabilized at 62 degrees. So we entered the front parlor and as we did, the motion detector went off in the vicinity of the back office. Pete went ahead of me filming the room and I followed behind. I turned around suddenly and grabbed my hair. It felt like someone had just pulled my hair!

"Freya, look." Pete grabbed my arm and pulled me toward him into the office. The mini chandelier was swinging back and forth and the chair that was facing the fireplace was now in the opposite direction.

"Are you getting all this on film?"

Pete nodded and we continued very slowly around the small room pointing the flashlight at the various objects and knick knacks on the shelves. Nothing seemed to be out of place. The room was cold but not like the kitchen. And the motion detector was still silent. As we left the room, I asked a question to the spirit named Sara.

"Sara? Are you here right now? Send me a sign again. Break a glass or pull my hair again."

Nothing happened. "Sara, are you the spirit who lives here? Are you the woman who cries in the basement?"

I could hear something that sounded like scratching. I looked around the room but couldn't seem to find where it was coming from. I left the office and went into the front parlor. The scratching was louder there. It sounded like it was coming from the floor. I bent down and listened.

"Pete, can you hear that?"

"Yeah, it sounds louder in this room. Check the EMF recorder."

I checked it and the recorder was barely registering anything so I placed it over the scratching noise. The lights start blinking so I placed my voice recorder next to it and began asking questions again.

"Hello, my name is Freya and I'd like to communicate with whoever is making the scratching noise. Why are you here? What do you want?"

"LEAVE US!" A loud female voice said as the chandelier above us swayed back and forth. Oh my God, she sounded angry. I took a few more pictures with my camera in the direction of the voice and the ceiling.

"Why do you want us to leave?"

Pete was standing behind me filming the fireplace and the rocking chair near the window. The chair continued to rock back and forth. I stood before the rocker and asked more questions of this obvious irate spirit. The rocker continued to rock back and forth, slowly at first but then, very quickly. Pete nudged me. I think he wanted me to keep talking.

"Why do you want us to leave?" I asked again.

"GET OUT! GET OUT! GET OUT! GET OUT!" Said the voice, but softer this time, in almost a loud whisper It was clearly a woman's voice and it seemed to be coming from the corner of this room. It was freezing now and I shivered at the sudden drop in temperature.

But suddenly, I could hear a slight crackling noise beneath me and then, everything turned to blackness and a feeling of warmth washed over me. I could feel myself falling and hear Pete screaming my name. The last thing I remembered was Pete reaching out to grab me as I slipped away, falling down deep into the dark hole far beneath me

.

Epilogue

"Sheriff, I just received an emergency call from the Regency Hotel on Main Street. Apparently, somebody got hurt during the ghost hunt over there. Call said a girl fell though the floor and landed on, now get this, a skeleton in the basement." Milly waited for the sheriff's response. She knew him well enough to know he was hoping for a quiet night since his vacation started tomorrow. It was a two week cruise of the Caribbean with his wife. Poor thing hadn't had a proper vacation in over three years.

"Call my wife and tell her I'll be home late," said the sheriff as he walked out of the station slamming the door behind him.

Oh well, just another typical Friday night in Agatha Falls, thought Milly as she reached for the phone.

If you liked my book, please leave a review online at Amazon.com.

Check out my author page on amazon and my blog on Goodreads.

I hope you enjoyed the book. The sequel, Murder on Main Street should be ready by next spring.

Thanks for reading this story.

Made in the USA
Middletown, DE
22 July 2018